À propos de

John Robinson

Table des matières

3

1 : Avant-propos

Note de l'auteur

Sans connaître le sens exact du mot, j'ai pensé que « Uber » était « là-bas » signifie, ou "l'élite". Un bon ami à moi Michael, qui parle plus d'une langue, m'a cependant dit que cela signifiait "au-dessus". Ce qui est bien aussi.

Probablement la chose la plus importante que vous, lecteur, voulez comprendre, c'est que bien que ce mot ait été détourné par l'utilisation de sociétés de location de voitures personnelles / de taxis (sans parler du service de livraison de nourriture de Macdonald), il a une étiologie beaucoup plus large.

et va plus loin que cette utilisation du nom.

Pourquoi ai-je choisi ça comme titre ? Bon, je dirais qu'en plus du conflit avec la langue qui est une idée assez cohérente dans mon écriture, c'est que j'aime à penser que la vie c'est plus que mes hospitalisations, mes divers crimes et autres délits et autres gimmicks. Erreur grammaticale sur la façon dont ma vie s'est déroulée.

Nous traversons nos vies comme des voyages. Parfois lentement, parfois rapidement, comme un clin d'œil. Et s'en souvenir peut être brillant ou douloureux. On va essayer quand même. Nous l'essayons avec nos familles, avec notre éducation et nos diverses occupations. Et travailler quand on peut garder un emploi.

La société est un effort collectif. Un monument commun que Milena a réalisé. Et l'effondrement récent du comportement civilisé à travers l'Amérique, causé par le massacre d'un Black Lloyd George, et la répression gouvernementale qui a suivi, montre à quel point nous devons aller plus loin.

Mais même si je n'ai pas le droit d'en parler dans mes dissertations universitaires, alors que j'aurais peut-être dû l'être, dans ce monde, nous signons un contrat à partir du jour où nous nous cassons les utérus en criant et en donnant des coups de pied, jusqu'à ce que nous atteignions notre dernière demeure. allongez-vous à la fin. Un contrat avec nos voisins, nos familles et nos communautés que nous utilisons pour le bien commun. Et si on rompait cet accord ? Eh bien, il y aura des conséquences.

Ce livre vole une photo, un instant, un seul souvenir, ou le temps où j'étais en garde à vue. Face aux questions des pouvoirs mentionnés ci-dessus et comment ils ont réussi à m'arracher les faits. En fait, tout en ne montrant qu'un seul instant, j'ai été arrêté et même détenu à de nombreuses reprises, et je peux utiliser toutes ces opportunités pour divulguer cette expérience à partir de maintenant.

Sans en dévoiler plus, voyez-vous comment vous l'aimez?

John

2 : À Votre Grâce

Un dimanche matin ensoleillé, JoJo
a été réveillé tôt par le téléphone.
« JoJo, nous avons un problème. Il
faut venir à la salle d'opération à
neuf heures. "Oh mon Dieu, je me
suis dit, de quoi s'agit-il, qu'ai-je
fait?

Alors, presque à l'heure, je
me suis habillé, je me suis lavé le
visage, je me suis brossé les dents
et .. . gauche de ma maison
..Ichich manoeuvré avec soin
à l'arrêt de bus et hésita bevorin la
bête en aciergrimpé
ichAls je me suis finalement dans
la villearrivée, j'appelais papa:
« papa, voici Joey Peuxtu me
emmener chez le médecin.? »

« Salut Joseph, pas aujourd'hui, je suis occupé, ce qui se passe? ai pas entendu cela depuis longtemps? »
« Oh mon Dieu, papa, vraiment? »
« Exactement! »

Alorsquand ilcommencé à pleuvoir, je boutonné mon manteau et me suis fait la demi-heure de marche jusqu'au bureau du médecin.

Quand je suis arrivé, le médecin est venu après un court temps d'attente de dix minutes hors de son bureau et m'a fait signe d'entrer dans son bureau. Là, assis Jack, mon infirmier, Pierre , mon père, et une trentaine de femmes inconnues...

" De quoi s'agit-il ? " balbutiai-je et tentai de reprendre mon souffle.

" Nous avons un problème, JoJo…
Ou plutôt certains d'entre eux… »
« Continuez ? » suppliai-je.
« Eh bien, pour commencer, qu'est-
ce que j'ai entendu à propos de
vous combattant dans la rue ? »

J'ai vérifié son iris pour de la
sympathie, mais je n'en ai trouvé
aucune…
"Tu veux dire la dispute que j'ai
eue avec Will il y a quelques
semaines devant ma maison. Celui
sur qui j'ai déchiré son manteau ?'
« Je ne le savais pas, mais que faire
ensuite ? »
« Attendez une minute, docteur B.,
ce n'était même pas un combat,
nous nous sommes battus comme
Randori. Will et moi avions tous
les deux une formation en arts

martiaux, alors nous avons juste
pratiqué nos compétences ? »
« Et vous avez déchiré son
manteau ? C'est une propriété
personnelle, tu vois ?'
"Attendez. Il m'a frappé à la tête. Si
je l'avais lâché, j'aurais été
grièvement blessé... J'ai réduit la
distance et j'ai essayé de le laisser
tomber par terre... Mais je ne l'ai
pas blessé.

Je suis sûr que j'ai arraché son
manteau, eh bien, il me l'avait
enlevé pendant un bon bout de
temps...
"" Tu l'appelles ton ami, et le même
gars qui a volé ton manteau ?
Qu'est-ce que c'est pour un ami ?"

"Bien sûr, le docteur Will est un
copain," essayai-je d'expliquer. «

12

C'est un copain donc ça ne me
dérange pas s'il vole mes affaires et
me signale aux autorités. Regardez,
il a même fait une vidéo du
combat, vous pouvez voir par
vous-même qu'il n'y a eu aucune
agression, aucune méchanceté… »
J'ai donné au médecin mon
téléphone portable avec la vidéo et
il l'a mis de côté.
Puis mon père a parlé… « Ou
comment c'était quand tu l'as
tabassé en ville, au centre de
Derby. Cela nous a été rapporté
par la garde de la ville, vous savez
? »

J'ai dit : « Mais papa, de quel côté
es-tu ? Je te joue aux échecs dans
les cafés Derby la plupart du
temps, généralement tu te laisses
gagner. D'accord, c'est peut-être

une liberté artistique, j'essaye de te frapper. Et je dirais échouer au moins les trois quarts du temps. Alors pourquoi me déranges-tu alors que j'ai le plus besoin de cette aide ?'

— Asseyez-vous, JoJo, répondit mon père.

« Personne n'est là pour vous avoir. Nous sommes tous là pour vous, c'est tout. »

« D'accord », continua le bon docteur. « S'il vous plaît, dites-nous plus sur ce qui est arrivé à votre ami Will au centre-ville ?"

« D'accord, docteur », ai-je continué. Cela n'a pas été filmé et il semble que quelqu'un l'a vu et nous l'a peut-être signalé.

» Bien sûr, continuez ? "

14

" Ouais, alors j'ai regardé des vidéos de Gracie Jujitsu que j'ai achetées directement aux États-Unis il y a quelque temps. Je ne pose même pas de questions sur les droits où j'ai dû payer les frais de port.

Quoi qu'il en soit, une grande partie de Gracie Jujitsu est un travail de base. Alors moi et Will nous sommes assis sur l'herbe et avons essayé certains de ces mouvements. Reach, évasion, prise,proximitéla distance (pour éviterêtre touché) et autres. »

« Et vous pensez que cela est un bon aprèsmidi passetemps dans le centre-ville? Estil pas surprenant qu'un spectateur ou un gardien vousmontré Has ?"

« Encore une fois, Doc, c'était de la part de deux adultes

consentants. Je ne comprends vraiment pas de quoi parle cette grande agitation ?

"D'accord" Dr. B semblait perdre du temps maintenant. « Je pense que nous en avons assez entendu. Puis-je me présenter à mes deux collègues ici... B est étudiante en soins infirmiers et K est assistante sociale. Si vous nous accordez quelques minutes pour discuter de votre cas, nous vous ferons part de nos résultats. P si tu restes avec nous, d'accord ? » J'allais dire papa arrête, tu ne vois pas ce qu'ils font ? Pourquoi ne peux-tu pas être à mes côtés pour une fois dans ta vie...

Mais ces mots sont tombés dans l'oreille d'un sourd.

J'ai été ramené dans la salle d'attente et quelques minutes se sont transformées en la meilleure partie d'une heure avant d'être finalement rappelé dans la fournaise éternelle d'une décision qui m'est restée jusqu'à ce jour.

« Joey, nous avons décidé de vous mettre dans la section un : un : sept des lois sur la santé mentale. Nous vous considérons comme un risque pour vous-même et les autres. Cela est principalement dû à votre non-respect de vos médicaments prescrits, des choses que vous avez faites et dites, à la fois avec et sans ce médicament. Se disputer avec des inconnus dans la rue et parler aux filles de la rue de positions inappropriées est à la fois offensant et potentiellement dangereux. Sans

parler du langage offensant dont
vous avez criblé vos livres au fil
des ans, de l'abus de confiance
jusqu'à l'abandon des noms et
d'une foule d'autres décisions
insatisfaisantes qui ne nous ont pas
laissé le choix. Nous vous volons
votre liberté et nous ne pouvons
que prier pour que vous appreniez
à vous comporter, et c'est si jamais
vous voulez sortir !
Vous serez admis dans un service
psychiatrique local avec la porte
fermée. »
À ce moment, deux policiers en
bonne santé et de bonne humeur,
sentant l'après-rasage, sont entrés
dans la pièce :
« S'il vous plaît ne combattez pas
JoJo, vous ne pouvez pas
simplement ouvrir le système et
attendez-vous à gagner ! »

3: Des pas de bébé à la victoire

Jetons maintenant un coup d'œil aux arts martiaux. la voie du kantana, budo

Mais il y a un dicton " joue avec le feu et tu brûleras "
Et en effet, quand il a incendié le premier pont, JoJo craignait d'être banni à jamais. En un instant quelque chose s'est passé Quelque chose s'était passé change en lui . Un morceau de son âme était perdu. Cette étincelle dans ses yeux avait disparu. Et à partir de ce jour, il a dû faire amende honorable. Pour essayer de combler la faille dans le karma

cosmique que lui seul avait causé
pour guérir les crimes. Et lui seul le
pouvait. Personne d'autre Pour
corriger pour eux les péchés de lui
et de ses pères et de leurs pères.
Ancêtres du père de son père !
Prendre son temps et prier. Guérir
les blessures de quatre générations.
Sur les mers et les montagnes.
Faire ce qui n'a jamais été fait
auparavant. Pour apporter la paix
dans le monde.

    Il appartient alors à chaque
être sensible de guérir, restaurer,
construire et représenter.

    Le mode combat commence
par de petits pas. Le premier
souffle pris par les premiers
peuples. Et chaque nouveau-né se
souvient de ce début. Alors place à
la victoire !

Le tournoi a été annoncé et a
rapidement démarré. Par les
canaux traditionnels et les plus
anciens par le bouche à oreille,
l'oiseau et le pigeon voyageur.

Peu de temps après, des gens
du monde entier se sont allumés et
ont testé leur courage à travers
cette épreuve. Certains prétendants
avec des capacités naturelles, de la
force, de la vitesse ou de la
discipline. D'autres sont revenus,
ont échoué, ont voleté et ont quand
même réessayé. Et encore et
encore. Jusqu'à ce qu'ils soient
battus et piétinés, ils s'enfonçaient
profondément dans les niches du
rez-de-chaussée. Pour qu'ils ne
retrouvent pas de nouvelles forces
et s'envolent à nouveau haut
pendant que l'éternel phénix lève

ses ailes au-dessus de la tombe de leur mort.

En effet, le Christ notre Rédempteur est revenu de sa mort. Certains ont perdu, d'autres ont gagné. Tout cela fait partie du jeu. Pour la domination, pour la survie. Et la gloire ultime.

Le match a été brutal. Des personnes sont mortes. Tous les jours. Les bonnes âmes retournent au ciel d'où elles sont venues. Tu viens de la poussière, tu retourneras à la poussière. Et les papiers ? Comment les médias populaires ont-ils expliqué ces morts sans précédent ? Avec une morosité sinistre et macabre, bien sûr. Parfois, la vérité était dite. Mais si souvent, entre la hache de la clavicule du boucher et la dalle de pierre froide de la morgue, la vérité est parfois remplacée par sa vérité. Et la vérité ? Perdu quelque part entre les livres des étudiants en médecine et leurs supérieurs, les conseillers et la police.

Même lorsque les coroners n'ont pas pu trouver de cause évidente, JoJo avait ses soupçons. Et il a juré qu'il ne sortirait pas comme un rat de laboratoire. Quand ils ont gazé sa chambre, il a dû ramper sur le sol, haletant. Demander du souffle et de la vie. Pas quand ils l'ont envoyé dans la cheminée ou l'ont enfermé dans l'isolement, couche après couche après couche. Il était venu jusqu'ici. Et il n'allait certainement pas laisser la Faucheuse l'arrêter maintenant. Pas aujourd'hui. Pas aujourd'hui.

La mort la dernière voie
Nous sommes nés. Nous vivons.
Nous mourons. Trois vérités
absolues. Si nous avons de la
chance, nous avons la chance
d'exercer une influence positive
entre ces valeurs absolues. Parfois
mais pas toujours. Nous faisons de
notre mieux.
Le Kung Fu, c'est bien plus que vos
pieds. Il ne s'agit pas seulement de
la paume de vos mains. C'est un
mode de vie, un mode de vie. Une
dévotion à une respiration positive,
une nutrition positive, un exercice
positif. Et si vous entriez en contact
avec de nombreux maux qui nous
hantent dans ce monde
postmoderne ? Prenez grâce et
réconfort. Personne n'a jamais dit
que ce serait facile. Mais pour ces
défis qui nous tourmentent, il y

aura le calme après la tempête.
J'espère que tu iras bien bientôt.
Plus facile chaque jour après le
traumatisme. La guérison prend du
temps. Cela peut prendre des
années. Parfois pour la vie.

S'il est vrai que je n'ai pas
encore à reproduire entièrement les
succès que j'ai eus sur la page écrite
avec ma propre carrière de
combattant. J'ai ma ceinture jaune.
Il a fallu un certain soin pour
atteindre ce rang, et je ne suis pas
sûr d'avoir jamais le courage de
prendre du recul sur ces tapis de
dojo. Mais même si non, j'ai eu ce
qu'ils m'ont donné. Et il y a des
mouvements qu'une fois appris,
vous n'oublierez jamais. Et j'ai
élargi mon répertoire. Du coup de
pied au renversement en passant
par les coups de poing. Comme je

l'ai dit, il y a beaucoup à
apprendre. Un autre avancement à
vie si nous avons de la chance.
N'ayez pas peur de vos ennemis,
qu'ils aient peur de vous. Et vous
seul pouvez le faire.

4: Lecrime ultime

service secret officiel duest délicat.
Il ne vous oblige pas à parler de
votre entreprise.
Vous ne pouvez pas parler des
personnes que vous avez tuées, des
missions que vous avez effectuées.
Les prostituées que vous avez
mangées ou les paiements que
vous avez effectués sortent du
cadre de la mission. Ce qui ne veut
pas dire du tout.

Pas à votre famille ou vos amis. A personne.

Vous souvenez-vous de l'espion d'il y a quelques années qui a été retrouvé attaché et bâillonné dans une petite valise dans son appartement. Et la valise était fermée à clé.

Cause de décès? Suffocation, suicide. Même s'il est physiquement impossible de nouer et de fermer l'affaire comme ça. Et je ne dis pas que ça. Un détective privé a été engagé et est arrivé à la même conclusion.

Il était clair que cet espion qui travaillait pour les services de renseignement britanniques MI6/MI5 avait dépassé ses limites... Peut-être avait-il rompu les termes de son contrat ou fait quelque chose qui était considéré comme impardonnable. Ou du moins embêter l'un de ces collègues ? Je ne peux pas le dire. Sans plus de connaissances, je ne peux pas apprendre plus de détails sur sa mort. Seulement que, si possible, il semble hautement improbable que cet homme se soit suicidé de cette façon. Mais sans plus d'informations, nous ne le saurons jamais.

....

Ou qu'en est-il il y a quelques années lorsque les "Phillpott", un homme avec trois femmes et une dizaine d'enfants, ont incendié l'appartement du gouvernement dans lequel ils vivaient et la plupart des leurs enfants, et maintenant enfermés pour toujours ?

J'ai du mal à comprendre comment il est possible pour un homme de faire cela tout en ayant sa propre famille. Je ne peux pas voir.

Veuillez comprendre que l'incendie s'est déclaré sur la boîte aux lettres de la porte d'entrée. Comme si quelqu'un avait versé de l'essence dessus, y avait mis le feu et regardé la maison brûler.
Le verdict officiel était que le couple l'avait fait pour réclamer une assurance. Mais si oui, pourquoi n'ont-ils pas sauvé les enfants et n'ont-ils pas fui avant de détruire la propriété ?

Je n'ai pas besoin d'évaluations psychologiques du couple pour déterminer s'ils ne sont pas aptes à être parents.

Tous deux ont pleuré devant le tribunal. Et qu'attendiez-vous Ces deux-là ont vécu une vie pleine et riche et sont indéfiniment en isolement cellulaire et ne reverront plus jamais leurs enfants. Qui pourrait demander cela à qui que ce soit, même à ses pires ennemis ?

Je comprends que le couple avait de nombreux ennemis qui étouffaient l'opinion publique, les réactions dans la presse et sur internet. S'il vous plaît, donnez-moi une minute. Tout ce qu'il a fallu pour un ou peut-être deux de ces ennemis était de jeter le gaz dans la porte et de s'en aller.

Personne ne saurait jamais mieux. Et il y a une conclusion finale au problème de Philpott.

Je sais que je peux me tromper, que cette opinion que je

viens d'exprimer n'est que cela. Cela n'est confirmé ou prouvé par rien d'autre que mon bon sens et mon intuition profonde. Les humains sont capables des choses les plus terribles, et le meurtre de ces enfants, que ce soit par un meurtrier inconnu ou par leurs parents, est l'un de ces crimes. Sans autre preuve, il s'agit d'un autre complot.

Quoi d'autre, la mort de la princesse Diana ? Les premiers atterrissages spatiaux des USA ? Tout le gâchis qu'était la (deuxième) invasion de l'Irak ?

Il y a plus de questions que de réponses, et il est facile de prendre une décision précoce sans aucune connaissance ou information préalable.

Chacun de nous doit
parcourir son chemin dans cette
vie et trouver ses propres réponses
à ces questions que la vie nous
pose. Certains d'entre nous y
arriveront, d'autres seront testés,
d'autres tomberont. Et pourtant, il
y aura ceux qui s'élèveront au-
dessus de nos ennemis, feront la
guerre par le feu ou la douleur, et
s'aventureront dans le nirvana
doré bien désolé.
Le feu qui consume et détruit est le
même feu qui lie et forge les
couteaux les plus tranchants. Les
couteaux qui décapitent les têtes
des tyrans des dictateurs du tiers
monde et des innocents. Cela
coupe les ficelles des mères de
nouveau-nés et achève l'émergence
d'une nouvelle vie.

Nous avons besoin des amants comme nous avons besoin des mères. Nous avons besoin de bonnes personnes pour se maintenir dans la communauté et la reconnaissance, des réalisations des autres et au-delà.

Il m'a fallu presque un an pour écrire ce livre. Il englobe un nouveau territoire, mais aussi un nouveau regard sur l'ancien. Je trouve l'écriture thérapeutique, elle me donne la chance de me libérer des carcans du monde vécu et de renaître dans le monde littéraire. Je me suis demandé si je devais essayer de trouver un éditeur, ou au moins un agent. Mais comme les deux précurseurs auxquels j'ai envoyé des précurseurs n'ont pas répondu, je repense maintenant le

concept d'auto-édition. Une fois
que j'aurai terminé ce troisième
brouillon, je verrai si je peux
terminer la couverture (telle que
conçue par un proche) et même
créer un dépliant promotionnel
Kindle Direct Publishing pour
promouvoir ce travail sur le
Kindle.

Je pense que l'édition finale de ce
livre sera bonne à lire et, espérons-
le, assez bonne à acheter. Je ne
pense pas à fixer des coûts de vente
élevés. Bon sang, je peux même
mettre les redevances à zéro pour
un potentiel de revenus maximum.
Mais ce serait bien de gagner de
l'argent avec cette version. Je bois
avec.

5 : Le contrat

« Lentement. Vous avez commis des crimes. Je sais que, vous savez que, vous n'avez pas derépéter. «
» Alors? "
« C'est donc une infraction grave. Mais comme je l'ai dit, nous n'avons pas à y aller.
« Quoi ? Peux-tu au moins desserrer ces chaînes sur mes poignets ? »

Un hochement de tête et une autre silhouette émerge de l'obscurité, et c'est fait.
« Donc, si vous ne vous souciez pas du génocide de masse, alors pourquoi diable me gardez-vous ici ? »

« Parce que... » a déclaré la Force..
« J'ai une suggestion à vous
faire... » « Je vous veux écoutez-
moi bien et ne répondez que
lorsque vous y aurez suffisamment
réfléchi, peut-être que vous
dormirez dessus... "
" Vous m'avez dressé les oreilles,
continuez... "
" Voilà... pour nous missionsnous
vous envoyons etdevenir un
employé de votre couronne? «
»si je refuse? «
» Eh bien, alors bien sûr vous
pouvez revenirarrière ... Retour à
votre excuse pathétique de votre
vie. Pas même jour après jour,
aucun Honneur, pas de
représailles… "
" Et si je suis d'accord ? "
" Eh bien, alors tu deviens l'un des
nôtres, en te cachant. Mais tu sais,

on ne s'attribue pas le mérite si tu
te fais prendre. Si tu te fais
prendre, tu paies pour tes crimes,
et cet échec, cette excursion, cette
dispense n'aura aucun motif en
cour ben ... il ne peut y avoir
aucune pitié pour votre type. Si
vous vous faites à nouveau
prendre, vous devrez payer. Les
quelques années que vous avez
déjà servies ressembleront à une
promenade dans le parc par
rapport à votre prochaine série.
Vous m'entendez. On ne joue pas !
"

" Vous ne jouez pas. Je
comprends... Alors qu'est-ce que j'y
gagne ? "
" Le sexe. Une évidence... De
l'argent... D'accord, bien sûr... Une
maison, un bel appartement dans
un quartier sympa, avec des

voisins sympas et sympathiques, un ordinateur portable, une plateforme de jeu numérique à la pointe de la technologie, avec une connexion et des jeux, oui, vous avez tout compris... Que voulez-vous de plus ? »

« Anonymat. Une cachette pour mes ennemis. J'ai échappé à plus de deux tentatives d'assassinat. Je ne sais pas combien de temps encore je pourrai tenir cette page...
"

" C'est fait. Je pense que vous n'avez pas bien compris comment cela fonctionne. Nous sommes les puissants, nous sommes vos amis. Et si vous nous polluez, nous vous attraperons et deviendrons votre pire cauchemar. Comment ça sonne ? "

Un temps, (une pause) et puis...

" Où est-ce que je signe ? "

6 : Problèmes dans la vie

Laissez-moi vous poser une
question... que dois-je faire ?
Ma vie semble s'être arrêtée, et
alors que je me tiens au bord du
précipice, je pense que je peux
entendre mes cloches sonner.

Je suis déchiré. Est-ce que je
bouge avec mon cœur ou avec ma
tête ? Est-ce que je fais la bonne
chose ? Et la bonne chose avec
Dieu ?

Nous nous sommes battus si
fort toutes ces années.

Mon phare, ma fierté, ma
joie.

C'est dur, tu sais, de dire adieu à
nos rêves. Faites comme si tout
allait bien avec désinvolture.

Le douteux JoJo avait-il toujours
raison ? Pour que les mensonges,
les doutes, les peurs deviennent
réalité. Que le passé n'a pas
d'importance, que cette incertitude
n'est que l'avenir que nous avons ?
  Tu dis que je devrais
m'arrêter et partir Prétendre qu'elle
ne signifie rien pour moi. Que cette
union est une perte de temps ?
Pour que j'écoute tous les ennemis,
les opposants et jette ce palais que
nous avons construit au cours des
dix-neuf dernières années ?
Même si j'ai refusé l'espoir il y a
très, très longtemps.
  Comment puis-je prétendre
que je n'ai aucune fierté? Que je

n'ai pas de coeur Que les blessures
du passé et les dommages déjà
causés sont des années que nous ne
pouvons pas récupérer.

Attendez, il y a un problème.
C'est la femme pour qui j'ai versé
des larmes. À propos d'elle? La
lumière de notre vie nous
maintient tous les deux en vie...

Qui a lutté lorsque leur fille a
eu une mauvaise grippe, je me suis
assis à côté de son lit pour soulager
la douleur jusqu'à ce qu'elle aille
mieux ?

Dis-moi de me taire
Dis-moi d'aller de l'avant
Ils disent que les enfants sont la
chose la plus importante. Ce
mariage n'est rien, un morceau de
papier.

Mais qu'est-ce que l'amour Partage quelque chose? La charge de la preuve d'une singularité ou le nœud d'un duo ? Nous nous séparons jusqu'à la mort.

Je dois rédiger mon testament. Je pense que j'étais à mi-chemin aujourd'hui. En fait, ce n'est qu'une question de jours avant mon trente-huitième anniversaire. Cette année-là, mon ancien meilleur ami, le sale Nick, n'a pas vieilli. Je dois le faire pour Nick. Comme il me méprise au paradis, sur nous.

J'ai assisté à ses funérailles et il dort maintenant. Nous rencontrerons tous notre Créateur un jour.

Je dois faire la bonne chose. Je dois mettre ma fille et ma femme au dessus de moi...

Je ne les laisserai pas partir.
Je dois rester forte, non seulement
pour moi ou mon amour, mais
aussi pour votre enfant. Nous
avons l'éternité devant nous. Pour
abandonner le passé. Mais
accrochez-vous toujours aux
quelques souvenirs heureux qui
restent.

Qui a dit que c'était facile ? Il
marque la fin d'une époque. La fin
d'un acte de la pièce et le passage à
un autre.

Quand je l'ai épousée et que j'ai
passé toutes ces années à l'hôpital,
je me suis assis à côté d'elle dans
mon cœur.

La fin d'une époque, ça va.
Un nouveau commence avec la
fermeture. Lorsque mes
médicaments fonctionnent et que

ma respiration devient plus forte,
je peux me faire de nouveaux amis.
Et nous, en tant que famille,
pouvons créer de nouveaux
souvenirs. Des moments de vérité
forgés dans le feu de la douleur et
de l'emprisonnement, libérés et
réalisés dans la félicité qui est
sérénité et force.

Un jour, nous quitterons tous
cette terre et retournerons vers nos
pères et ancêtres et nos mères et
autres ancêtres. Nous devons tirer
le meilleur parti des mains qui
nous sont présentées. Les
personnes que nous rencontrons et
les relations que nous pouvons
entretenir.

J'ai été pris dans un piège à
miel une fois. J'ai décidé d'aller au
poste de police et d'écrire ma

version de l'histoire afin que si jamais cela se produisait, je me souviendrais déjà de l'événement. Cela a été fait par un inconnu qui m'a dit qu'il avait déjà obtenu des condamnations de plusieurs personnalités de haut rang de cette manière. J'ai eu de la chance que ce ne soit pas moi.

En fait, quelques années plus tard, j'ai découvert qu'une personne qui avait installé ces pièges à miel sur les réseaux sociaux s'était emmêlée. Je suis convaincu que cet idiot a ce qu'il mérite.

Après ces événements horribles, j'ai couru vers des gens qui m'ont saigné à mort pour tout ce que je valais. Je prends à la fois ma santé et ma fortune et presque mon mariage. Dieu merci, ces moments sont terminés !

Qu'est-ce qu'on fait maintenant? Je dois développer mes forces. Certes mon écriture, mais aussi ma lecture. Continuer à payer mes factures et mes cartes de crédit jusqu'à ce que je ne doive plus rien. Pour continuer à soutenir mon autre significatif pendant qu'elle continue de me rendre visite. Et entretenez de bonnes relations avec mes autres parents et amis du mieux que vous le pouvez. Cela devrait suffire.

7 : Qui suis-je en train de combattre ?

« Alors, où allons-nous
maintenant, JoJo ?
Quel est votre plan, votre objectif,
votre objectif?
Qui est ton ennemi ? "
" J'ai vu Shadow comme mon
ennemi... "
" Qui est-il ? "
" Du noir. Non, pas ça, pas lui... "
" Pourquoi pas ? "
« Eh bien, j'ai rencontré quelques
hommes noirs-africains-anglais
dans les salles. Et ils étaient cool.
Généralement des gars sympas.
Bon sang, je suis même allé en
Afrique de l'Est et j'y ai passé
plusieurs semaines dans un
département verrouillé. Et
l'équipage était assez
extraordinaire pour moi. Bon sang,
je me sentais comme un roi. Tu

m'as bien traité, bien. Je comprends
que ...

» « Donc, si ce n'est pas « Shadow
», qui?

» « Eh bien, le National Health
Service m'a gardé derrièresalles
fermées pour beaucoup trop
d'années malgré son apogée, je
veux dire plusquatre ans, où j'étais
' serviteur" de leurs soins. Bien sûr,
ils ont peut-être fait de leur mieux,
mais comment oublier ces années
qui m'ont été volées ? Je ne peux
pas les oublier, encore moins leur
pardonner d'avoir volé certaines
des meilleures années de la vie.
Bien sûrle monde continue comme
jamais, maismien est coincé. »
« Sans donnernoms, tous ces
conseillers etjuges ethommes
etfemmes qui setournés mes
tourments en en secondes,

minutes, heures, jours, semaines,
mois et enfin années les les mêmes
bâtiments, les mêmes lits, la même
nourriture et les mêmes chambres.
Quel était l'intérêt ? La grâce, la
guérison ? Où était la protection ?
La logique, la raison ? "
" Je ne peux pas oublier, encore
moins pardonner. "
"Le mieux que je puisse faire est
d'essayer d'avancer. Pour que ce
soit un succès pour le reste de ma
vie, pour les années qui me restent.
Encore et encore. Te vaincre en
faisant quelque chose de ma vie
s'ils vient de me radier. C'était un
peu un combat! "

8 : Université

« Alors, que faites-vous
maintenant ? »

« Comment pouvez-vous
progresser, sans parler de guérir, là
où il y a une pression pour être
performant ? »

« Vous pouvez considérer qu'au
cours des trois dernières années de
mon cours de cinq ans, au cours
duquel j'ai fait mon baccalauréat ès
arts spécialisé conjoint en études
théâtrales, je n'ai jamais été
autorisé à monter sur le podium.
En fait, je disais catégoriquement
que *alle* Teilzeitstudenten, waren
nicht ausführen dürfen. Schon ein
paar Jahre später lernte ich eine
weitere gemeinsame ehrenamtliche
Theaterstudentin kennen, die mir
erzählte, dass sie genau das getan
hatte: die Schauspielerei in der
Jahresproduktion des Jahres."

„Es zeigt sich wieder... Es ist
eine Regel für einige und eine
andere für alle anderen! Ich hatte
ursprünglich gehofft, dass mein
Theaterausflug mir einige
dramatische Live-Auftritte bringen
würde. Was ich weiß, wäre
schwierig gewesen, denn mein
Gedächtnis ist wie ein Sieb, so dass
ich Schwierigkeiten gehabt hätte,
mich an die Zeilen zu erinnern.
Ganz zu schweigen davon, dass
meine Atmung schwer zu
bewältigen gewesen wäre, wenn
nicht für mich, dann sicherlich für
die anderen Darsteller und das
Publikum."

„Wenn ich eine Sache von
meiner CollegeKarriere gelernt
habe,ist es ziemlich vieldass alles
wat ze je vertellen onderhevig
heißt aan voorbehouden,

uitsluitingen en Ad-
hocvoorwaarden."
,Begrijp mich alsjeblieft niet
verkeerd. Het maakt wel uit de
hoeveelheid werk sterben je erin
steekt. Het is belangrijk dat je de
boeken leest, de online
tijdschriften, en goed kunt
opschieten met je leeftijdsgenoten."
„Verwacht niet dat de docenten je
werk voor je doen."
"Verdorie, ik kreeg zelfs twee keer
te horen van mijn begeleider dat ik
het Konzept van mijn Proefschrift
moest nalezen."
        „Ok, ik heb wel een cijfer van
68% weten te halen voor mijn
eindscriptie Dat een ist sterke twee.
Één, en het was op basis hiervan
dat ik kon afstuderen met een
hogere seconde. Maar stiekem
hoopte ik op een primeur voor

deze krant. Door een of ander
wonder. Ik zou het krijgen, veel
werk, lezen, onderzoek en steken
original, kijkend erin geestelijke
gezondheid/schizofrenie vanuit
een lekenperspectief."

„Met inzicht, met *het* inzicht
dat wordt verkregen door jaren op
de gesloten afdelingen te hebben
doorgebracht. Dat geeft de positie
van ervaringsdeskundige mij af te
komen.
"Dus nee, ik koop het niet.
Natuurlijk niet. Hoe kan ik? Maar
in het proefschrift moest ik
academisch blijven. Dat betekende
niet alleen mijn diepe haat tegen
het hele psychiatrische apparaat
omarmen, althans niet expliciet
zeggen.
"Het werd eerder een
onuitgesproken waarheid. One

onderhoud, positie. een hand,
range, een verdediging. "
"Verdorie, mijn hele study was een
functie. Een gezamenlijke
inspanning, tussen het doen van de
lezingen, het bijwonen van de
lessen, schrijven en presentaties,
tot een keu, een thee, een par, een
aasvolu .kte, niet mijn module.
Verdorie, ik denk dat mijn
modusgemiddelde over de vijf jaar
een derde was (40%). Maar er war
zo'n spreiding in de behaalde
cijfers, van een laag derde tot een
top eerste, dat het mediane
gemiddele was .en twe : één. Von
voor een ander woord, a *goed*
Diplom!

„Ik ben afgestudeerd en dat
is het bewijs dat hard werken
loont. En als ik het niet goed kon
vinden met de docenten, dan nam

ik ontslag bij het accepteren van de derde cijfers sterben ze mir gegeben. Gaf mich onvermijdelijk."

"Dus, wat kunnen wir leren van dit proces?"

„Ik zou zeggen dat hard werken loont. Verwacht niet dat je een Diplom op een bord krijgt. Zeker niet op Derby University. En je moet proberen origineel te zijn. Neem het niet als bewijs van de feiten sterben je wordt verteld. Wees voorbereid om de waarheden die u is aangereikt, en die u al vasthoudt, in twijfel te trekken. Je kunt je eigen weg banen op dit gegeven. Doe je eigen onderzoek en beraadslaag en creëer je eigen inzichten, op welk gebied je ook hebt gekozen om te lezen.

Het lijkt veel op taal, of *Hegemonie* zoals Gramsci zich ooit

ontwikkelde. Die Agentur, die
einzelne Akteure, von Politikern
bis hin zu einflussreichen
Akademikern, auf das Feld und die
Strömungen und Strömungen
innerhalb dieses Bereichs
beeinflussen können. Wir alle
hoffen, nach unserem Tod in
Erinnerung zu bleiben. Und nicht
für die falschen Dinge. Und auch
wenn wir alle irgendwann
vergessen werden, bedeutet das
positive Einflüsse und Eindrücke
zu Lebzeiten zumindest, dass wir
hat einen Unterschied, für das Wohl
der Welt gemacht.

"Lesen. Das ist wichtig.
Teilen Sie Ihr Wissen und Ihre
Entdeckungen mit Ihren
Mitmenschen. Im akademischen
Sinne Ihre Kollegen und vor allem

Ihre Vorgesetzten die
akademischen Dozenten."
„Machen Sie sich keine Sorgen,
wenn die Art, wie Sie schreiben,
nicht allen gängigen Normen und
Protokollen entspricht, die Sie an
anderer Stelle in Ihrer
Universitätskarriere füttern."
„Wir haben alle unseren eigenen
Stil. By attending your lectures,
and reading most of the texts set,
and at least some of your
secondary readings as well, you
earn the right to speak, think and
write, in your own voice. This is
your privilege. Everyone has their
own style.

And the academic habitus
(world), is an eternally evolving
and adapting world sphere. With
norms that are constantly adapting
to the latest generations of students

and academic papers, and new excellences across the board. These are the pinnacles you need to aim for!"

"So, did you deserve your grade?"

"Well you know, I tried my best."

"I worked hard. Even if compared to my generally younger peers, my work may not have been that impressive."

"But I did as much reading as was physically possible, spending many hours in the library, and not just playing Facebook poker (although I did this as well). I even managed to grade for my yellow belt, at a local martial arts club, in my second year. Although I had to give this up, when I found my martial studies were taking too much out of me and decided that in order to complete this education,

I was going to need to give it my one hundred percent."

"A dedication which eventually gave me a voice, written, and an ear. An ability to seek out and find the truth from studies, with revelation, and compare and complete."

"So, what else should we be aware of? What should new, and returning university students know, what advice can I give you to support your own role, and position, in this eternal struggle for pole position?"

"As I have already said, you need to do the work. Attend your classes, and don't just think that because there is nobody there to penalize you for missing classes, that your attendance won't reflect in you grade. Because it will."

"Something I haven't mentioned prior, is that your relationships with the academics. I have already said you need to build bridges with your peer group. And they are going through pretty much what you are traversing too. So, if you ever miss a class or two dues to ill health (or a hangover), they will be the ones to turn to, for lesson notes."

"It is how well you get on with those that are grading your work, will be what makes the difference between a good grade, a great grade, a pass and a fail. If they don't like you, then it is going to make it that much more difficult for you to achieve a top grade when the marks are issued."

"And no, there is not room for recourse."

"Are you sure?"

"Okay, let me give you a final example on this issue, before drawing this discussion to a close."

"Go on…"

"In our final year L a young white, European student was headed for a good first, except her final theatre play-script, was failed by a (new) lecturer, who seemed hell bent on making her own stamp on the class of 2016, by marking the student down."

"She was forced to completely redo and submit her dissertation/play, several thousand words, in a completely different style. Which was now capped at a pass (a low third). Consequently, bringing her final grade down to a lower second, and thus, as she related, stamping out her dream of gaining a masters, either here or at any other university across the country."

"So why do I think she was awarded this low grade?"
"I think because she had chosen the 'Theatre of the absurd', as her plays genre, which aims to test the audience's preconceptions of drama, with extreme and sometimes outright absurd convention breaking ideas... And the unit leader, didn't appreciate this..."

"Just as I submitted an essay to this tutor and was failed. Which basically meant I had to put in an overcharged second essay, to bring the grade up (it was averaged across the two units), to scrape a third overall."

"Was this being fair?"

"No. But I think I understand how it works? Basically, what it amounts to is this… You are the student. You are there to learn. You do what you are told. The lecturer is above you. Hell, they like it if you bow down to them like gods! They expressly don't want you to come up with *original* ideas for your undergraduate degree. Even if you thought that was the goal you were aiming for."

"As the fee payer, you need to satisfy their requirements." "They are the ones who will be grading your work. And each essay, is double marked, so you need to pay attention, to what you are told in class. And give them back both the same ideas (content) and styles you have learned (form)."

"And remember, you are going to university to learn. To develop and improve. If your sole purpose is to spend the three years of your attendance going out drinking, clubbing, and having fun, then you will fail your degree (to say nothing of the hangovers student nights out are renown for!)"

"Equally, if you expect university to be an appendix of A levels at sixth form, where the standard of your work is as uniform, only second to the dress code of your school, you are similarly going to struggle."

"University, in effect, gives you infinitely more free time, than A levels ever did. But it is expected that you use if not all, then at least half of this time, for self-motivated study. So that means yes, going to the library and reading books, yes going on the journals, and extra internet research (which will become ever more important as you journey ever closer to your final year.)"

"And as for medical students? Well God help you. There is that much more pressure to perform, at a consistent high level, across your studies for this discipline. I was lucky to get into university in the first place, much less a STEM degree. But the fact that I did get in if anything drove me to attend and work hard come what may. I once even heard that one of my lecturers accused me of cheating across my units… She said I hacked into other students' computers, maybe if they had been left open, and stole documents. Which is the biggest load of bull I've ever heard. I didn't once cheat at my degree, not then, not before. It's something I have never done, and never plan to do. It's like telling lies, I simply don't do it. Suffice to say, that was another one of my lecturers, who gave me no grades better than a low third. Silly idiot!"

"I'm not saying *don't* enjoy yourself. Sure, go out the weekends if you want. But equally, give yourself some leeway in your approach to writing the work. And reading. Read around. Make time to explore the reading and explore your own writing styles. And when the papers submission dates loom, give yourself a good few week, a month even, to stop drinking, and get down to the *hard graft* which is for first few drafts."

"Finally remember university is only the first step in your graduate life, which will hopefully take you beyond the realms of your previous meagre existence, and jettison your way above the stratosphere, where other mere humans reside. You are going to be a graduate! You are going to have letters after your name? Well done!"

9 : Graduation

"Okay JoJo, so what can you tell me today?"
How about we talk a little bit about getting a degree?

"Okay go on, so what can you tell me about this then?"

Okay one step at a time... Firstly you know that I got my degree? And I'll go to hell if it wasn't a challenge. But both of my parents have one, as does my sister, and so you might say it runs in the family...

So, what tips can I give you? Firstly, work hard across your years at university. At first it may seem like years of luxury, seeing as most of the student time is given to reading. And how many young undergraduates do this? But don't be fooled. Take this free time as an excuse to slack off at your peril. Because if you do, when the final essays are being written, and exams taken, and you are struggling with some of the concepts being asked of, you will only have yourself to blame.

Hopefully you can use this time given, to read, in the library and at home.

Oh yes and here's another useful piece of advice, don't be afraid to buy the books on your reading list.

Whilst it isn't expected for you to read every single book on the reading list, cover to cover, you are expected to have had a good read, of at least one of two of them per unit. You also need to become familiar with the student resources (ergo journals) available to you. This is my impression anyway. Please understand that I am only one individual who conquered the system. At least managed to graduate. But I hope that some of the pointers that I picked up along the way, can be of benefit to others who are in the process of doing so. Most of all, don't give up! The number of students who I have seen start the degree, and *not* finish, is quite alarming. But hopefully with my careful guidance, and your hard work, you will be able to avoid becoming one of these statistics!

There is a great amount of literature and knowledge out there. Make the most of it. Something I tried to do is to read at least a chapter (thirty pages or so) every day.

Don't cut corners. By the time you reach your third year, you should become a competent enough reader/writer, to be able to slow read when needed, and fast read, for the rest of the time. This is a skill that comes with time. And please pay attention to your text. Learn how to take notes, and then take notes during your lectures. Write these up on the same day when you get home.

Like I said, most of the undergraduate time is given to self-motivated study. I'm not saying you shouldn't let your hair down, every once and a while (the odd weekend for example). But for me, the truth is that the only time I went out clubbing, was after I had completed the damn thing. This was due to a combination of the fact that I was so preoccupied with the reading, and simply didn't have time. I also didn't have the friends to go out with. Then when the opportunity presented itself, I did finally let my hair down, get drunk and spend far too much money on getting other people pissed too. But that, you can say, is another story.

Student life should be some of the best years of your life. You will meet a great number of young, and eager to learn minds. And, a great wealth of expert knowledge, presented to you by your lecturers.

A trick I learned whilst on my studies, is that every lecturer, will have his or her own separate expectations of you, as to what is required to achieve a passing grade. Assuming you do what is asked of you, for example the readings, and engaging with your classmates, for the units studied, then you can expect to get a passing grade.

And if you want to exceed this? Well do extra reading. As I already mentioned, pay attention to the journals. Don't be afraid to read too much, or do too much research...

Near the end of my degree, I remember somebody told me, that undergraduate work is only supposed to present, and deal with the knowledge already out there, and it is only when you reach the peak of postgraduate (masters and doctorate level) research, that these engaged minds are hoped to create new knowledge...

Yet when I was studying for this degree, every essay I submitted, especially for the final year modules, were novel ideas.

Facing an unknown horizon. And I really loved reading these challenging new texts; from Apartheid era African drama, to powerful Shakespeare, to founding Feminist Education ideas to an engaging third year Sociological class discussion. Which all really tried to put a hundred per cent in. And developed my reader's voice, to create new ideas never been previously known. I hope so anyway.

By staying with me so far, I hope you have come to value my way with words, which I took to my essays. So, whilst it is true at school, they may teach us to write in the third person to stay objective…

I still used the first person (stream of narrative), to carry off my essays off. And whilst I only hit the sixty eighth percentile for my final dissertation, which was disappointing because I was hoping to get a first (which is seventy percent or above). On reading it back, I noticed a few spelling errors, which will be what stopped me from getting the best grade. I should have listened to my supervisors who told me to proofread the darn thing! Oeps.

I was still over the moon to graduate…

Most undergraduate degrees take three years, with the exceptions for Law or Medicine, which take more. However, my degree took extra time, partially because I did a blended study (of part time, and full time). And partly because I had to take extra units, to cover the fact that in my second year, I had switched to doing a combined program, of Theatre Studies, on top of my Sociology major.

The experience on completion has been one of intellectual wealth. And financial poverty. I am very pleased that I met the people I did meet, across the time. Had the conversations I had and read the books I read. But I am still paying off the debt I owe. Which has now breached twenty-five thousand!

You should be warned that you might meet the odd lecturer or two that you don't get on with. Academic doctors who, despite your best efforts, only give you passing grades for their units. I sure had a couple on my program. And it is a shame that people like this, still get lecturing roles, today, when if a student, puts his or her whole into his work, this study should be respected.

But don't let them get you down. Life is not always meant to be easy. We are set these obstacles to test us. If you can continue to do your readings and research, continue to engage with the work you are set, and continue to give it your all, you should hopefully have enough decent grades to carry you through to a good grade overall.

So yes, your degree will be a challenge, it will test you. Don't think that the somewhat inviting work you ease through in your first year, will continue in the second and third. Without shifting up gears. The work does get harder, and you will soon need to learn to up your game, to succeed. But don't let this defeat you.

If you keep up with the readings, and the in class and out of class discussions and subject engagement, you should do just fine. We develop as thinkers and readers, and the process is a rewarding one, if you stick with it...

I have given you some tips in today's entry, on how you can prepare, and ultimately complete your degree, with as best as I can. So, whilst it will be true that every degree is different, whether it is your sole aim to get a good job,

perhaps in teaching, or another
profession, don't let the workload
overwhelm you. Don't give up,
even if it seems like you can't get a
good grade, even if you must
retake a unit or two. Persevere
forwards. I will be right there
beside you on graduation.

10 : Insomnia

So, what do you want to talk about
today?
I've got to be careful.

I'm holding on to some
things, whilst still trying to get out
every day.

I still like listening to music
and playing on my games. Even if I
must be careful that they don't take
over.

I was able to get voluntary work, after I finished my degree. Although that packed up after six months. And I have had more than a few driving lessons, although I decided to hand in my provisional license after my latest admission into hospital.

God, I hate those places. It's like every time I go in, they keep me for years at a time. And that's no lie.

I go in, and I see other people go in and leave. Again, and again, and again and again. These people will enter and leave, and I will still be there. Silly idiots. How do they want me to forgive them for this? It's almost as if they think I am a risk to the world, whereas I am under the impression that all these medications they give me, only makes the problems worse and not better.

I can't prove this, but there we are. I don't like it how they say I am going to have to take them for the rest of my life. I don't like that at all.

So, what are the side effects, apart from putting on weight? Well it kills my sex drive. Which is proved by the fact that when I come off them, I am like a wild tiger, damn.

And what else? It slows down my speech. Again, when drug free, I speak faster. Wat nog meer?
They make me like a zombie. They reduce my strength and decrease my motivation for getting out. Hell, I used to walk everywhere, but now I can't be bothered to.

And they cause sleep disturbances. Something like insomnia. So that I must be careful not to be up in the nights, and in bed at day. This could be down to a poor routine, and I can fight it by getting up on time and going to bed at reasonable hours. Yet even this seems to be a struggle.
I love my sleep. But it is rare for me to get to bed before midnight even if I want to. Sometimes, I go to bed early, then wake up when it is still dark, unable to get again to sleep. So, the poor cycle continues.

I didn't lie on my benefits application form. I do have problems with engaging with people. And I also have other 'life' problems, which persist despite me being out of hospital. If anything, they continue, because of this.

11 : Progression

It was a big step for me, to escape those golden walls, and return to a space I can call my own. I used to like playing my games. On the Xbox One, and I still do. That alongside with meeting my dad, wife, and other friends. And listening to the music, I don't really have that much time left over. It's like how my consultant wants me to get another General Practitioner. Yet I haven't done so. I told him, "I am too busy". So, he responded "Busy doing what?"" Watching YouTube music videos?" "Yep" I answered.

Curse them. Who do they think they are? Hell, what has a

General Practitioner ever done for me? Apart from pretend to shake my hand, and give me a fake smile, whilst they pretend to listen to my rants.

What do they want me to do? You know every time I enter hospital, it takes a General Practitioner's signature, as well as a social worker's, and a consultant. It's bull-crap.

I know as much about my own health as they do. If these guys were so smart, then they would have 'fixed' me, within a few weeks of admission, instead of keeping me on and on.

The same goes for the consultants, damn them. I wouldn't even have one of these, if given the chance. I have learned about the 'rule of thirds', which is one third of inpatient admissions, will only have a brief stay, and then get out and get better. Another third will be admitted then get out and eventually get better. This will take longer, but they will do it, nevertheless. And the remaining third, will remain on drugs and sick, for the rest of their life. With only medication keeping them, 'well'. My community nurse tells me that I have already fallen into this 'worse' category, by the evidence of my long-term stays.

These professionals keep me in locked wards and don't like the fact that I know more about my own mental health than them. In this case why is it that when they give little privileges such as the ability to leave the ward, as a first step, and then the ability to take myself to town, and eventually have leave to sleep at my own flat, that I'm able to make much better progress and recovery, then when I'm trapped on those damn wards day after day? It stands to reason that the little exercise and fresh air, associated with this extra freedom a section seventeen brings, will of course be much better from me, than being trapped in that stupid cage!

These are things that belong to God. Not man. Not a man who thinks himself God. Not any doctors, or professionals, who think themselves, the warders of men. Damn them. They've never been my guardians. Prison guards, sure. They know how to lock the

ward's doors when I am inside
them.

They even supervised the
theft of my laptop, which held lots
of valuable, and pretty much
irreplaceable chess lessons, as well
as the original digital copies of my
books. These guys took that. Or at
least one of the patients on the
ward took it, and one of the nurses
co-opted with them to ensure they
got the computer off the building.
Not to mention my mail was
repeatedly opened and the
credit/debit cards stolen, along
with the pin numbers, and I lost
thousands from the accounts in
this way!

Damn them.

I'm not saying that my writings,
were good enough, to be published

at the stage of first draft, they were when he took it. But that isn't the point. So, when quite recently, I tried to buy some advertising for their documents, the payments were rejected. One said it was because I didn't have the book title on the cover, but the other didn't even have a decent reason. Which for all we know is because the content has already been published elsewhere.

In fact, believe it or not, but I once found a significant portion of my first book, in another famous author's novel. Stephen King I think it was. And we are talking word for word plagiarism here. This was for 'JoJo's Amazing Adventure and other short stories. Of course, I would hardly be able to claim copyright over it because that guy has millions and would beat me in any court case. I also know how he got hold of the manuscript (that first draft I sent to a scandalous so called publishing company, and the contact I had over there said he never received the memory stick I had posted to America, only an open, empty envelope).

So, this is how the document was stolen, and later copied, most likely sold to Mr King, for God knows how much?

So, what next? Hopefully I will be able to continue working at this book/novel, for such a time as will be enough for a reader to engage and swim with it. New ideas, suggestions, and currents, carrying me along. With my own life's journey being upheld within these windows of pages. Like mirrors, they can catch the light, as well as moments, to a decent progression and conclusion. Finishing when the natural progression of this narrative reaches its close.

12

The police detective didn't look amused

…

"Okay JoJo so what do you want to talk about today?
Your crimes?

….

"No but you've already signed the waiver?! This is out of your hands…

…

"What have you done which is so special? What have you achieved that makes you *so* good, that you think anyone will want to read?

"Talking about Ninjas? Ha!
How can you be a Ninja, when you can't even walk three steps without wheezing for breath?

"Or computer games? No man come on, that stuff is for children!

"What makes your little world so compelling, that it will have dreams any higher than the average man. Or woman now we come to think of it?

"So, what, you have read some powerful authors in your past.

"That doesn't give *you* any precedent!

"If you want to be original, and I very much hope you do, you're going to need to start knocking down some of the walls, which you have erected, to reveal areas of your life, that you have previously kept standing.
"And you can't do that? So how are you going to write a bestselling novel?

"Sorry what was that? You say, *everyone* has limits?
"Like teachers *can't* teach outside the curriculum.
"Or lawyers *can't* discuss their other client's cases, with others, without betraying their confidence?

"Or how surgeons and doctors, *must*, uphold the Hippocratic oath, in their actions on graduation, to do no harm, and serve the best of their ability, to the welfare of patients universally?
"Not to mental patient confidentiality?
"You mean that? How a soldier, must obey orders, or face court martial?
"Is that what you mean?

"You really think you can write a whole novel, off the back of your subconscious leftover raggedy mind and subliminal *souvenir* base. (Which means *memory* in French. ed)

. . . .

93

"What gives you that impression?
What gives you that right?

....
"So, you have written before, yeah,
I get that....
"I see that you have got a degree, a
good one for what it's worth. Well
done. Many people don't have.
"What seems to make you think
that your grade, is somehow
superior to those others who don't
have this?
"That you brought your bride over
from another country. Goed voor
je.
"Shame you couldn't hold on to
her for more than a few years, here
in this country....
"That you are so sick, that you are
forced to take an injection every
month, for what would seem like

94

the rest of your life. Goed voor je.

"How does this change things, in any little way?

"In fact, how is a mental illness something to be proud of?

"Unlike the other people, who get sick, take meds, then get well and come off them. You have been on these medications for Fifteen years now, and there is a good chance that you will never get off them.

"Yes, I know it is your intention to break free of this choke hold, but really? When every other time you have come off them you end up relapsing…

"I know the social predicaments, not to mention interpersonal ones, have troubled you in the past at the same time as your breakdowns.

"But the fact that you have now

spent over five years on locked
wards, means that the odds are
stacked against you I'm afraid.
"Other people get it, get better, and
get off their drugs? Yet you get bad
and go downhill way too fast.
"Every-time.

"And so, what, you met a senior
police chief in town, a couple of
decades ago, who offered you a job
in the police, for you to turn it
down, without due consideration?
"Even if I were to believe that this
did happen, despite your
protestations, how does this give
you any head room? You didn't
take the job; you didn't get the
promotion. You haven't done it?

"You what? You lost what? To
whom? Taking how long? Sex you

say. Wat is dat? I can barely remember. And it doesn't matter? Suit yourself. Seems like with the rest of the world you are preoccupied, so how does this somehow make you an exception?
….

"And you are holding on to what? With whom? What oaths are you striving to respect when you already broke them a long time ago?

"JoJo. JoJo. JOJO! Listen to me kid. You are a joke. Your entire life is built on a Vernier of falsehoods and misinformation.
"You are a *keyboard* warrior. You think that just because this book, has taken a kick-off from your many thousands of failed, online

appearances, that this digital fame somehow crosses over, to the real world? Well let me assure you son, that it doesn't.

"Why do you think it is you can't get a job? Why is it do you think that you are still many thousands in debt £££ to these credit card companies?

"Come off it our kid. You really think that level of debt, is an accolade not baggage?
Wo gehst du hin? You live alone. You suffer cycles of delusion, and stupid relationships with people you have met, and are probably never going to see again.

"You think that this world is the only one?

You think that we don't have to
pay for our actions?
That your child is not going to miss
you when you go?
That the world will not be a better
place, when your miserable
specimen, stops leaching off the
state, and the state provided
National Health Service?

"Come on our kid.
Start taking responsibility for your
actions.

"For all those people you have hurt
with your actions, all this needs to
be answered.
You thought you were the centre of
the world.
And then you made up some lame
excuse, that at the centre, is the
pivot. On which the rest of the

world rotates. You struggled to get
your degree. And then when you
finally got it, you struggled to do
anything with it.

"So, you finally say, that you have
set the imprint, lit the touch paper,
for your daughter, to walk.
Opened the door, for a child, to
walk through. And you think that
this is going to be any easier for her
when she grows up?
That she won't have to face the face
hurdles and barriers, in her
transition, to adulthood, that you
are undertaking, just because you
have been there yourself?

"You think somehow that her life
will be easier, just because yours
was hard?

"Hard life? Don't make me laugh.
All you do is sit on your bum all
day and drink coffee in town?
What is so hard about that?

"Who cares that you didn't have
any friends at school? Who cares
that you failed at Physical
Education?
"Who cares that every partner you
have ever had, has walked away
from you, rather than be dragged
down by your self-pity and
commiseration?

"Who cares man? Not us…

"So how about I start putting some
ticks in boxes, whilst your story
remains unfinished?

"A downwards trajectory. Your crimes are such, that it is going to be impossible to ever see any future meaningful employment. And so, what you have joined a gym? All you are doing is adding stress to that already shattered heart."

"And my child, what about her?" JoJo whispered.

"Sure, we all hope that she does well. Hope that she makes something of her life, that she can graduate, and that you will be there to clap on her graduation, the same as she was there for yours.

"But don't think that she won't have to walk through the barrier. Walk the pit of fire, which scars as it does whittle down the numbers of those who can, to those who cannot.

"And her accolades, and achievements, will be hers alone. We can't take away from one another's victories but must build on our own. And this goes to everybody from the future king of England, to the lowliest beggar on the street. God help them.

"An intergalactic game of chess. This is fifty shades of ember. Real life with real people you are playing with, real hands, minds and hearts. Just because your body works like a zombie doesn't give you the right to drag down everyone else around you…

"Please take a step back now and let others with their whole lives ahead of them, take precedence in the roles you were unable to see through.

"A Forty year old man, with no car, no house, and no job. And for the time being at least, no wife and daughter! Things are not looking good, are they?"

JoJo said nothing

13 : Martial Art

Okay. I want to get thematic for a bit. Let us talk about martial arts? So where does my training and knowledge come from?
    I first studied Judo at secondary school. I didn't rank up

at this point. For the two Judo
gradings I should have gone to and
passed, I flunked out of both.
Calling sickies. Which was a bit
lame, but then seeing as my
secondary school education was
just that, lame, then why should
Judo have taken me above this?

But I did learn two things
from these lessons. Firstly, how to
'break-fall', which is how to fall, or
take a throw, and prevent yourself
from damage on the landing.
Which is very important in martial
arts? This applies to any fight,
where you stand a chance of being
thrown.

How you do it, does depend
on the attack, but the basic premise
is this : You cast your hand and
arm out to the floor, before you
meet it, ahead, so that on the

impact, your upper limb, takes the force of the impact fall.

You must ask yourself as the opponent, which would you rather, be hit by a strike, or be hit by the world, which is what's going to happen by a throw. Also, should you find yourself in a position of attack, against a single adversary, having the power of Judo, which is control, throw and pin, is a very effective repertoire. I'm not saying you can step into the Octagon, and start winning Championships, with this single repertoire alone. But for the 'street' and self-defence in a real-life confrontation, it is very good.

Wat nog meer? Well the second thing I learned from these classes, was the act of communion. Something, I was never able to properly capitalize on, in my youth. And it wasn't until my adult hood, hospital and then university life, that I was properly able to demonstrate and build on this knowledge. But the simple act of being in a training hall, with other likeminded learners, and to learn, listen, build, and develop, is so important for me. And for the next generation, which is why schools and teaching are so important. I really take my hats off to teachers their job is so important and building up the knowledge and confidence of the next generations, remains one of the most important foundations our society has to offer.

.....

I have of course learned other
important martial lessons across
my life. So much so that my second
(A Patient in Time : JoJutsu) and
third books (Fighting Madness),
take prime position in staking this
claim, and building a foundation
for my martial world.

It seems to be that the
internet, now so heavily guarded
and moderated, that anything that
senses novelty and originality, and
steps outside of the norm, is
heavily cast out too easily in my
opinion. It seems to be very
difficult to create something new,
in this world where who has the
biggest wallet, seems to take
precedence over everything else.
That's not to say that you, as a
newcomer, don't have a chance to
make it in this world.

Sign up to your local dojo, be it Tae-Kwon-Do, Judo, Karate, Kung Fu, Aikido, Kickboxing, Boxing, Gracie Jiujitsu, Judo or Jeet-Kun-Do. Just be warned that ego and pride in martial arts, seem to be heavy. The odds are that your sensei/master/or teacher, will expect you to honour and bow down to him (or her), from the get-go.

They want you to do well, but to conform, and if you do step out of line, or use your martial knowledge outside of the dojo/ring, don't expect more than one warning before being kicked out of the club. This is my experience of it anyhow.

So, what now? You can continue to learn from outside the ring. When you have conflicts with your opponent's/enemies in real life, it is good to have the knowledge that you can defeat them in fisty cuffs, should things reach that stage. Obviously, you want to avoid this from happening. The same as your goal should be to walk away from confrontations before they arise. Or let the professionals/police etc. deal with the worst situations before you must. But it is good to have some knowledge, and direct powers, to fall back on, should the need arise.

So, what other moves to I know? Well probably the next move I have in my arsenal is Ikkyo. Which to sidestep, and then swipe, the enemies attack. I first learned this from my aunties' boyfriend Danny when I was still living at my mum's house about the year two thousand. Danny was a high black belt in his own style of Karate, which he had several dojos opened in his unique style of Karate, across Britain and Ireland and Africa. Danny taught me Ikkyo, part of how to escape a grip. Any grip will always take place in one of four ways. On top, thumb under. Or on top thumb over. And then under thumb over, or thumb and fingers over. This may be difficult to visualise, but if you can get a friend to grab your arm or wrist, and you should be able to practice these moves for yourself.

The breakaway Danny taught me, uses the knowledge, that the thumbs, are the weak point of a grip. And then, when attacked in this way, you can pull your hand free, using the other hand, and an awareness of the grip. Or even simply by twisting your offended arm, in face of this first digit, skill and movement, will enable you to escape, without even needing to use the second arm.

Should however you be grabbed by both arms, then to my knowledge, you will need to use both arms to generate the power of the breakaway needed. Depending on the strength of your adversary of course.

So, what else do I know? Well homage to the late grandmaster sifu Bruce Lee, I've got his one-inch punch down to a par as well. I even did a YouTube video of this at one point, although I think I've since taken this down. And we are taught in Aikido never to attack, at least never to be the aggressor. But this move, the one-inch punch, was something I skilled in, before Aikido. And literally is another skill. I developed this, by punching walls, be it in a police officer holding cell, or outside. And again, this is not something to be taken lightly, and I have also never been told to do this voluntarily.

I think there is a whole martial world dedicated to throwing, and receiving punches, namely Boxing, and Kick Boxing, both of which I only have limited knowledge of. When you develop as a martial artist, and when you develop your own experience and skill range. You will be opening doors. So that, should the occasion arise that you are forced to defend

yourself, you will have choices, options on how to react.
Throwing a punch, or an Atemi, can be one of these.

Something else I would like to mention, another facet of my martial repertoire is footwork. Watching the placement of the steps of your opponent, can tell you a great deal. And this is best practiced, not so much in the ring, as it is from walking locations, from A to B.

I realize that as we grow older, and hopefully procure and later master use of the four wheels (driving), many people get out of the habit of excessive walking. But don't become so lazy that you never walk anywhere. Because footwork, in fights, and conflict situations especially, is very important in telling you, how your opponent intends to act, and how best you can position yourself to react against him. Or her, should you be a woman fighting a woman.

Wat nog meer? I also want to stress the importance of DVDs and books. Whilst it is an ideal to train in a dojo, with others. And to develop yourself for competitions, should the opportunity arise. It is also good to read and watch others, from the static media, on the occasions that you can't attend class in person. Or even as well as. I will aim to create a list, with some brief descriptions, or martial arts books I have read and can wholeheartedly recommend, at the end of this book, so you can take heed from these, should you so desire.

I think that draws to a close this brief if important lecture for today. There is much more I know about this field, but it is quite hard to summarize, and capture in written form, without freezing up. Or running dry.

The world of martial arts and discipline is such a vast one, and indeed one which I have only touched in my life, as well. But respect and discipline, are the key concepts you should honour, in your practice of it.

There is a term called Budo, which means 'The Martial Way', this is something that all martial arts clubs, I've ever been a part of, respect and seek to honour. The one's I've been allowed to join that is at least!

In their practice, and teachings. To honour your teacher/ sensei/ sifu/ master, to honour your style, and your family, your community, your country, and ultimately to honour man (and woman) kind!

So be punctual for your classes, trim your nails, and stretch before classes and so on. Veel geluk.

14 : Stopping smoking and a fight

Okay. I've done what I said I was going to do. Read a few chapters of the brilliant book *Easy way (by Allen Carr)*. And you know what? Yes, it has helped me stop cigarettes. By carefully walking down the path he narrates for us, I now feel comfortable in the safe role on non-smoker, again.

I need to be careful. No more, picking up the nub ends off the floor. No more urges for the odd pack or smoke. This is my health, and future we are talking about here. I have gone about two weeks now I think, without a cigarette. If anything, I owe it to my daughter, to stay off them.

So, what else? Last night I got in to a 'fight'. With one of my mates. Even though it was less a fight, then randori, which is a controlled battle/bout, between two willing opponents. Like we agreed, beforehand, to stop whenever one of us asked.

And I already had it in my mind, that I wasn't going to hurt him. I didn't want to throw any blows, merely control him, and maybe get into the clinch.

Well what happened, is that I grabbed him, and held on to him. He escaped, but then I was able to grab him again. I ended up ripping his coat, and I ripped it worse the second time I grabbed him. I think it was my coat he had stolen off me anyway, in the first place. So, I don't feel too bad about mashing it. Even though I did offer to buy him a McDonald's to make up for this. And don't mind buying my friend a meal.

So, what else then? Did I tell you that yesterday I got pinked, and then banned, from one of the martial arts websites, I used to be a member of. I have a big problem with them doing this to me.

Despite what my dad says (that the internet is full of nonsense, and is only bad news for me), I did used to enjoy logging on to this site. And chatting and laughing with my friends there. And so yeah, I was upset when they banned me, for what must be the fourth time from there.

But I've no intention of going back there. It is unfair what they've done, to pink me (which is a temporary withhold of posting privileges), followed by an outright ban within twenty-four hours, and no spark point, or reason, to trigger this. Damn.

I need to switch my lifestyle from a night stalker, to one who walks in the light. Or in other words, to start getting up at decent hours. But it's hard. Once you get caught in the trap of going to bed late, then even if you want to go to bed early, the body fights it.

And even if in some ways I am strong willed, such as able to complete a degree, and not miss any lessons due to sleeping in, that was hard. Now I am past that 'hard' part of my life, I am not in any rush to force myself up every day. There just seems to be no need.

These days, I also must get up for my injections, once a month, at the hospital. I normally must be there for ten thirty AM, and sometimes my dad gives me a lift in, so that helps that. But I still struggle, and I need to sort it out, so I can restore some sort of normality visiting my immediate family, which I can't do when I am asleep all day. To be continued…

15 :

"So, JoJo", the police constable continued,
"We heard you have been getting in to fights again. This is not good. This is looked down upon. You do realize that we now, as a school, conduct a zero-tolerance policy to fighting. Do you really think that your borderline knowledge of martial arts gives you a license to fight? A license to harm, a license to kill.

Because it does not. If anything, that yellow belt should have taught you about discipline, restraint. Instead you act like a bull in a china shop. Bullying these poor hapless individuals before you. And if any one of them should ever stand in your path? Ever say no, well god help them!"

……

"Let me ask you a question… Can you please tell me about that list you drew up a few years ago? You know the one you wrote when you were severely unwell? Very psychotic?
I heard it was a list of your enemies. And a random selection of their friends on the internet? I heard it offered rewards, bounties on their heads. That you contacted 'Anonymous', and with your rudimentary knowledge of computer and hacking skills, ordered their execution. That some

of them went in to hiding, and that some of them were terminated?"

"Do you really consider this a good use of the stock market funds? To execute random people, who some little troll gets upset by? You call yourself a sniper? Then you use an AK-50 in a crowded room. With the doors and windows barred. So that some of them must go in to hiding. And not everyone makes it out alive.

What gives you the license to conduct this kind of operation? You say it was you against the world? You say you didn't like their attitude towards you? You said that they would pay for what they did to you?

And we tried to order your assassination. Sent a message to an operative, giving them your description, and executing the target? Except it didn't work! Instead the message was relayed to your address, giving you pre-emptive knowledge of the strike, and a wariness which allowed you to call it off?

Or maybe it wasn't your power which cancelled this order, but we considered your circumstances, the good will and support you have showed in looking after your daughter and wife, and decided that you could do more good alive, then dead.

That your head will help more on top of your body, than off it?

You do know that you are on your final warning. And that if you ever consider it right to break the rules again, we won't hesitate to

act. And this time the two years
you last spent in detention, will
seem like a walk in the park.

You have been warned!"

16 :

Relax, survive, and get better.
Okay guys and girls, youth, and
elders. Take your time. This is your
adventure, your journey.
It's not a race. Even if sometimes,
you will need to win your own
battles.

Listen to your own songs.
Make your own relationships. You
can't win every battle. You can't
win every fight, without taking a
blow or two. Losing a cut or two, a
scrape or two.

The world is changing. Back in the day, not everyone would smile. In photographs. I was one of the first to smile.

I remember posing for a police mugshot, and then smiling for the camera. Nearly all the perps who get their profile's taken didn't smile. But when they took mine, I made my grin from ear to ear. Funny really. Laughing out loud.

I have started reading a new book. *Sacred contracts* by *Caroline Myss*. She talks about the religious founding fathers, Abraham, Jesus, Mohammed, and the Buddha. She says that these powerful people, each initiated, and fulfilled their heavenly contracts, starting in their late twenties, but then realized coming on to their thirties.

People have different trajectories. Must go through their own battles. Different levels of knowledge, Sophic gnosis. Learned from the Christian Goddess, Sophia.

So, what now? Relax. Survive. Get better. I am under the impression that these medications I'm on, kind of make me into a zombie.

When I saw, one of my good friends a few days ago, she said that she thought that I was very unwell. But when I have seen my professionals recently (mental health nurses and consultant), they all said how much better I looked.

I guess it's all relative. My friend maybe hasn't seen much of me since I have come out of hospital ten months ago. So, she doesn't have an accurate base to judge me off. Maybe that, or maybe now I am quite unwell. When I look in the mirror, I see big black lines under my eyes.

At least I have stopped watching porn on my computer. That stuff rots the mind.

So, what else? I'm struggling with this stop smoking thing. I haven't had a cigarette in about a month. But I'm on the vape stick. Which provides me with lots of replacement Nicotine. I would give this up as well, except I'm not strong enough too. One day hopefully. I'm also finding it hard to get the energy to walk into the town. The buses from my local stop are so regular, it is hard not to hop on the bus with my gold card, at every opportunity.

I think when I next have my medications reduced, if they are that is, I will get some energy back. Get some powers back. Get my appetite back. Have my insomnia, and sleeping routing improved. Able to focus better on games better.

Give up smoking better. Also get my sex drive back better. I don't know what they are putting in these drugs. But I am sure part of it is a medical castration. Don't forget that the last time, I got out of hospital, I was able to go wild with my Johnson, and then I also spent lots of money, on my credit cards on hookers. Now I am in debt. So, I just must stay on top of these, pay off my debts. And take it easy.

Good luck!

17 : Desperate

Yeah so there we were. She had left me, and I was desperate. Talking to the strangers on the street.
Smoking drugs. And somebody knocked me out.

"Wow, that must have hurt?"
Yeah, it's kind of did. Do you want to know the story?

"Sure, go on."
So, there I was on the streets of Derby litter picking. A useful skill I learned from my secondary school days.

Anyway, I came across a broken Budweiser bottle, on the street, next to a bus stop. And I was picking up the bits of glass. Then this big black guy came up to me and kicked it out of my hands.

I shouted "Oi" and "What do you think you are doing?"

And I can't remember what he said. If he said anything at all? Only then I started picking up the glass again. And by this time, my hands were covered in cuts, from the glass.

Then like a real idiot he came up and kicked the bag out of my hands again. This time rather than attempting to diffuse the situation verbally, I went up to him and pushed him on the chest.
Big mistake. In a flash he sparked me out, (he punched me hard in the head, enough to knock me clean out).

I might have survived the punch, had it been daytime. But because it was midnight, and pitch-black, I was knocked out cold.

Some people told me, when I was in hospitals after this, that I should have ducked. But I wasn't ready. And he got me.
Anyway, I woke up in an ambulance, and a police officer told me that they have him in the back of a meat wagon (police car), and asked me if I wanted to press charges...

A beat...

I considered it but told them that I didn't. Told them to let him go.

He probably deserved a criminal record for what he did to me. But I'm not a grass. Plus, you could well argue *I deserved it.*

Anyway, they took me to hospital, and I waited on a hospital bed, with the live Emergency Room taking place around me. And then I walked out. Because I don't like hospitals. And it's not like there was anything they could have done for me.

I went back to a friend's house, but she turned me away. Then I went to my dad's place, and he called an emergency psychiatric assessment on me, where they unanimously agreed to have me sectioned, from July 2017 to October 2018, two years. I think I must hold the record for lengthy inpatient stays in hospital. In the UK anyway.

Anyway, the professionals took one look at me and put me on a section three (six months) no messing about! So whilst most people only do a *week or two* in there, I did nearly *three years!* And it wasn't the first time. Damn.

Well we need to look at the positives. So at least when I left, I had managed to procure a nice new flat, in a new part of my hometown, Derby. And I have also applied, and been accepted for, a decent amount of monthly benefits. Which I fully deserve, seeing as the state owes me this, given the amount of time I did locked away. I even spent six months of my admission, in Bradford. Which was difficult, seeing as I was a smoker again, by this point, and in Bradford, on the acute ward, you weren't allowed any cigarettes, then on the less acute ward, we

could have two a day, for most of
the time. And I think this may have
been upped to four a day, by the
end. But it is so different, between
having your freedom, and being
restrained to the will of others.

Therefore, I harbour such
amount of hatred for certain
people. Such as my dad, and my
community nurse, and the various
consultants. Because these were the
people, who were responsible for
my detention, and I find it hard
forgiving them for this.

They still treat me like a little
boy, even though I am thirty-eight.
Where has my life gone? But at
least I have a family, which
includes my daughter. And they
mean the world to me. Many
people go through life, without

ever having been able to hold on to
what I have...

Whilst it is true, that I haven't
been able to hold down a job, or a
career, and my degree, I am now in
a nice flat with weekly meetings
with my stepdaughter. And if I
have learned one thing from doing
it, that's how to do a degree. So,
know if my children want to do
one, which I can recommend, and I
can also support them through it.
Something my parents hardly ever
did for me.

When I was a child, I didn't really
have any friends at school. And
when I got my GCSEs, I really
couldn't see a future. In hindsight, I
should have gone to college, and
made friends there. But hindsight
is a fine thing. Which means that,

unless others can share this
knowledge with us, we must learn
the hard lessons in life ourselves.
Learn the hard way.

I did eventually go to college,
four different colleges in fact. As
the years rolled by.

And in 2005 I faced my first
admission for mental health. It was
messed up. I have been in and out
of hospital for many times, since
then. It's 2019. But I shouldn't be
hateful. I have got a loving
separated wife, and daughter. Who
I love to the ends of the Earth, and
I don't need anyone more now that
I have got these two?

I don't really talk about them
too much because it is private
information. And none of your
business. But they are the yin to
my yang, and I still value their

input tremendously in my life,
especially now that I have my
freedom back, and can see both on
a regular basis.

18 : Never forget this

Take a big breath. And let us take a
step back…
"Where are we going today?" Ren
inquired.
"I want us to move forwards… and
I want us to move backwards…!"
JoJo provided.
"But how is that possible, JoJo".
Ren was stumped. This perplexing
oxymoron sent the Ninja's head
spinning.
"By the power of the spoken
word" JoJo suggested. "Don't be
worried about time. We are going

older; this happens every day. But those books of mine you discarded…"

"Yes, what of them?"
"I want us to revive them, to remind them. Those epic fables, of Chinese and Indian parables, let's hold on to them?"
"So, you want to rewrite them?" Ren inquired.
"Maybe. But let us just hold on to the past. This younger generation, the Millennials, where would they be without the building blocks our ancestors provided for us?"
"What building blocks?" Ren was still stumped.
"Ever heard of the French revolution? Where the generation of the future, discarded the old (ancient) regime of the past?"
"Um hmm".

"Or how about the pyramids,
those giant miracles of
achievement".
"I'm not here to trick you Ren. I
want us to work on these projects
together. Like we did before".
"Just like the good old times?"
"Just like the good old times."

So how do we start the stories,
where does it begin?
It begins with a young child called
JoJo. JoJo was exceptional, for what
he was not. Bands made songs
laughing at his name. And when
he sat down to write his first book,
all he could think about was
stealing!
"Really, that's quite a poor excuse
to write!"

"I know" JoJo scolded, but there we go.

"He also had dreams, dreamed of flying away to exotic countries, becoming a man, and bringing back his bride..."

"Wow, that sounds juicy", Ren lifted.

"So, did he ever succeed in this aspiration? or was he forever a stalker of the night?"

"A stalker of the night, night stalker? What the hell are you going on about Reynold?"

"Oh, I don't know".

"Anyway, back to our protégé, he wasn't a night stalker, whatever you meant by that confusing query. He was however an insomniac, and a menace. As a child he didn't have any, friends at school. Or at least none that would

be able to save him from the black hole he was about to fell into."
"Then after completing his GCSEs, but before collecting the results he was hit by a car, crossing the road. From this he broke his neck, and was in a controlled, induced coma for ten days!"
"Wow, so he broke his neck. Wow he is lucky to be alive!"

"I know Ren. You're right."
"What happened next?"
"He started visiting the library and he found two books to love and cherish. He had not actually been able to do any reading in hospital, and so holding down the attention to finish these books he had found, was difficult at first. But he persevered and succeeded."

143

"So, what were these books about?" Ren continued.

"The first was a book of Indian short stories, and the second was a book called "Concentration and Meditation", by Christmas Humphreys".

"So where does the Chinese influence come from then?" Ren seemed unhappy, unsatisfied.

"Have you ever heard of Bruce Lee?"

"That epic Chinese martial artist? Wow, of course I have! Who hasn't? But where does he come into this narrative? I thought we were talking about your character?"

"I am Reynold. But hold on. I remember staying up late one

night, at my mum's house, and watching Bruce Lee's last complete, and epic film *Enter the Dragon*. And then walking a couple of miles to a park, at midnight. I don't know if I had a weapon with me, a Jo staff for example. I don't think I did. Only a hessian bag. Anyway, I walked this long distance to this park, near my local university, from which I would graduate from some twenty years later."

"JoJo", Ren took a deep breath. "But what has this got to do with writing?"

"Well" finished JoJo, "after watching his films, and fighting my own fear of walking long distances in the dark, I also brought Bruce's first complete book, 'The Tao of Jeet-Kun-Do'".

"And?"

"Well this martial arts Bible, suggested many of the moves, and power, that this character had. And was also close to my beginning footsteps, into the martial world. Not just the images, but the ideas. That one man can take on the world. Like he did, or Nelson Mandela, or Jimi Hendrix, or Mohamed Ali. Or Joan of Arc. Or John F. Kennedy!"

"Some powerful names you have cited there. And so, from this vacuum you were able to find inspiration, and direction?"

"Something like that".

"The powerful heroes of the past, as well as the known, and some unseen heroes of the present, have protected your life, ever since the day you died. And whilst you still have problems, you need to see each day as a blessing, hold on to the treasures that your friends and family give you every day. Say thank you for these blessings, and everyday do your best to make the world that little bit better. This is your responsibility as a son, husband, and father. Please never forget it!"

19 : Moving forwards

JoJo took a rest.
Who was he?
Ren took a rest. Who was he? He was JoJo's friend. He took a ride with him. He followed him over the mountains. Read his books. Listened to his music. Accepted his

mistakes and visited him when he
was in hospital.

This life isn't always easy.
Sometimes the devil throws sin at
us. Smoking cigarettes, drinking
beer, and watching porn.
We need to try and cut down on
these errors. Cut down on our sins
and build an acceptable life. And if
we don't? Then Karma will hit us
in the ass.

We need to love our families,
our partners, our children, our
friends, neighbours, communities.
And lastly our enemies.

Drink coke. Drink coffee. Drink
milk. I don't know what else to say.

Try to write. Write essays,
write books. Build networks.
Speak languages. Build a life, with
what you've got, not what is

presently inaccessible to you! Wat nog meer?

JoJo has a history. Not always positive, and he doesn't know if he can undo the damage that he's done. But he is trying.

20 : A Glimpse of Games

Sit down. Sich beruhigen. We all know why you are here. That's not the problem. This isn't just about you. It's about us. What can we achieve?
The world has changed. Forget 9/11 and 7/7 It is no longer Goliath against Samson. Too many tears have been shed. Too many lives have been wasted.

So, here's the deal. You work with me, and I will work with you.

You work for me, and you will get paid.

You look after your family, and I will look after you.

You revise the texts, your texts. And I promise I will read them.

Damn right they don't make music like this any-more.

Good old Shadow has rinsed that gene pool for far too long, for far too many innocents wrought.

There is no longer a thing called good luck. The books have been traced, and beggared, fixed, for too many millions.

Walk your damn mile. The hangman's isle. You did the crime; you do the time. There is no such thing as immortality, and if you cross us you will be dropped faster

than a fat man toilet brick. And
that's the nice way of saying it.
There is a network. And viruses,
spread faster than a stingray in the
Galactus.

I don't care about your
training. I don't care about your
stimulus. This isn't then, this is
now.

Take the internet. Break it.
Put it back together again.
Break it again. Fix it again. Break it,
again. Fix it again.

Do we see a pattern arising
here?
You know chess? Great play me.
Prove it? You don't learn it. I will
teach you.

You think you are good? Beat
me… You want to lose to me?
Great, do so. The world is your

oyster. Damn I learned that
rubbish in school.

That and chatting up girls.
Who I didn't stand a chance with?
But I've made my quarter mill.
Spent it. Now save it again!

Drive. Fly. Play. Lose. Win.
Vote, abstain… Where are we
going here?

I'm driving in the night, tonight.
Proper ammunition. I'm down
with the refugees.

And for all those criminals
that steal our time? Damn you.
Who do you think you are playing?
God?

He only had one ring. On the
ring finger? And his mother,
Mother Mary? What about Mother
Theresa?

Hey, you should I slow down? Nah kid drive fast. Just cos they got a badge they could still be imposters. Lyrics from the Fugees debut album the Score. They don't make em like that anymore. As I already stressed.

Do you know what I missed the most when I was in hospital for those long years?
Freedom? Yep. Freedom to walk to town. Yep that as well. How about fresh air?

But you know what. I've learned a lot from hospital. And it's not just been about chatting up the nurses. Although that did help.

Making friends. Engaging with different energy wavelengths. Eating different foods. Dining like a king, from a rationed menu base.

Wat nog meer? You're not getting out. Not after what you've done. And when you do get out, if you ever do, we will keep you on such a tight leach that one slip up, one criminal misdemeanour and we will have you back in that cage faster than a fat man who sat down to fast. That's fatist. Lol

So where are we headed. Deep into the night. Across literature. Music, books, a glimpse of games. And on a very rare occasion, a movie. Now who would think that your best friend would be your worst enemy, and your enemy your best friend?

21 : Hacking

Calm down. Relax. You will pay
for your crimes. We all do. Karma
catches up with us in the end.
Do you want to know a skill, that I
failed to learn at school? Making
friends. I didn't learn that at
primary, and I did not learn it at
secondary. Do you know where I
learned it? I learned it in hospital.

As the days rolled into
weeks, months, and now years…
Well at about the months stage,
there's only so much soul, and wall
gazing, that one can attend to,
before you must relate to the
residents. The guests. Guests of
honour. And no difference if you
will never see them again, you will
pick up medals along the way. My

life savers badge, which I got from saving a woman from the brink of death. She saw angels on her bed and went into cardiac arrest. So, I waited until to spasms stopped, before giving her mouth to mouth and chest compressions. But that's a different story.

So, these crooks, psychiatrists, and their minions, they can steal the best years of our life. But now that I have passed the halfway mark, of my 2054 destination, what do I have? What do I have to show for it?

A family? Check... Some internet friends. Rekening. A few books to my name, check.

Wat nog meer? A portfolio, check. Which is growing by the quarter.

Martial arts? No. Not really. I have been bitten by one too many snakes, on my road to the next belt. It is a mainly misogynistic and ego driven world, that these black belts don't want to be driven off their horse. I'm not saying that it's all bad, just the ideas of rules, and martial laws, do as much to spit out, rather than engage with new ideas and people.

I've got my own style, my own movement! Which you would have known if you read my second book and third books!

So, what else. A couple of addictions, which I can't shake for the life of me. At least this time I seem to have got rid of my porn addiction. I can still visualize sex without having to watch it on the

screen each time I go to sleep.
Adult discretion advised.

With the help of the internet, I am
learning things about the CIA, John
F Kennedy, and the Vietnam and
cold wars, that I never knew
before. I like hacking the systems,
because I am using my hacking
skills, first broke with Uplink (an
indie PC game of twenty years
ago), to give me special insight into
these missions, the game revolves
around. And it would be easy just
to say, "oh yeah, it's only a game,
all of that is make belief", which I
would be tempted to confer with, if
it wasn't for the fact, that these
computer files seem pretty legit.
    The only part of that system I
haven't been able to crack so far is
the numbers. So, some of the

ciphers are letters (just strings of apparently random letters). However, cracking that is easy, all you must do is go out into the root directory, and type DECODE (followed by the letters of the cipher), and it will provide the message.

However for the numbers, and just one guy figured this out on the internet, you have to have a key to the cipher, specifically, some paragraphs, from one of JFK's books, which is on the desk of the woman who is questioning you in the opening cut scene.

Take good care.

22 : Zombies

It's all in your hands young Jo.

The past. The future. The present...
So, what you've made some
enemies? Play with fire, and you
will get burned.

Only this time, not this time.
You are going to live another three
score, give or take.

So, your alias, 2054, is that
when you are destined to live
until? What is the significance of
the numbers?

Ik weet het niet zeker. I kind
of selected them because it seemed
apt at the time. And then some?

Or Chess, or Poker, or
Supercity? Or Tekken, or Call of
Duty, or Skyrim, or Grand Theft
Auto, or Black Ops Three?!?

Or two paracetamols to take
the edge off the pain. Even though
you're not in any pain.

How about your psychiatrist
calling your dissertation bull crap,
and publishing it in an academic
journal?

Yeah that sounds about right.
'Damn him', that's what I say.

I hope he gets paid enough
money, to say that kind of stuff.
Where's the gratitude, where's the
sympathy. Oh yeah, sorry I forgot.
This is the twenty first century, we
don't have time for that nonsense
out here.

Forget your crimes, forget
your history. Forget the pedigree.
This is the new world. Survival of
the fittest. Like I said damn him.
Damn the lot of them.

So, what else? Where do we
go from here…? The other day one
of my support workers, told me
that he is reading one of my books

(the second one, A Patient in Time), and he says that he thinks that I am a really good writer, he asked why I'm not writing any more...

That is positive thinking, and its people, and thoughts like that, that motivate me, to sit down, and write, like I am doing here. God bless him. You know who you are...

So, what else?

Anyway, eventually two of the guys died, but I held on. And the main man, even revived me four times. And I even revived him once, and so that was why he was being kind to me, I think?

It was quite instructive watching this Alpha player

running like mad, from the masses
of the undead, as the level opened.
We killed lots of these undead.
And he had a nice and powerful
automatic rifle to do it with.
Eventually he died, and then it was
game over. But I think he got us to
level 24, which for those of you
knew to this Zombie Apocalypse,
is a worthy feat.

It is nice playing Call of Duty
Black Ops with my daughter, and
with other online enthusiasts, and
not bad for a game, which is
coming up to twenty years old. I
found that out today, by reading
the back of the box. To think of all
these years I have missed out, on
the visceral gore of the undead.
Mainly due to being locked up, for
reasons largely out of my hands.

But therein lies some other stories. And gives us ammunition for another day? Or another book? Or maybe I have already wept another about the past, in my four other books. We need to think of some new ideas, for this one, I dare say. Peace out.

23 : Do Not Jump to Conclusions

Time, control, and patience. Protect those you love. Attack those you hate. Try to find a happy medium between the two.

Like zombies for example. Put a bullet between their eyes. Make money.

Play games. Enjoy them. Watch
other streamers, online, via
YouTube or Mixer.

Take your time. Compose
yourself. Eat. Exercise. Do Martial
Arts, if you can find a dojo to enter,
and a Sensei/master, who will train
you. And doesn't take over their
class with their gregarious ego.

Vape. And then one day
switch to the Gum!

Don't drink, don't smoke. Try
to avoid eating meat. Cook, do the
laundry, hover, tidy, and wipe the
table down. Make your bed. Wear
fresh underwear every day.
Pray. Mediteren. Live a good life.
Make good friends, on your
journey to the grave.

Watch YouTube videos.
Make your own streaming channel.
If you care to? Watch others.

Have a family and look after
them. Avoid unlicensed
medications. I once thought they
were the bee's knees, until I
overdid it, and got burnt.

Don't pester the police, but
contact them, if you think you are
worried for your safety. Stay
within the limits of the law. *Don't
drink and drive.*

Wat nog meer?

Study. Write. Write a journal,
blogs, online chat, and your own
book, if you can?

Take your time. Balance.
Learn how to play chess. Learn the
names of the pieces, their values,
the three stages of the game. And
how to convert an advantage (be it
material, positional, or driven

initiative) to a win. Take a draw, when offered, and you *don't* have a clear advantage.

Play Call of Duty Zombies. Black Ops 1 and 3, both have great zombie minigames. Kill zombies, before they kill you. But don't be afraid of dying. Because the zombies will kill you eventually. There are too many of them. Literally an unlimited supply. So, the zombies, will win in the end. They always do. Just be sure, you send a good number of them back to perma-death, the second time round!

Make good friends. Stay in touch with them. Make new friends but treasure the old. For they are silver, and these are gold.

This world is ours now! But be aware, we are going to someplace else after this one.

Repent your sins. You will not be in control anymore when this life is over.

Which direction you are heading to, up or down, well that is up to you. And don't think we live separate lives. We are all connected to one another. And our families, and our friends. And we are connected. Try to save yourself. And in the process, save one another.

Do not jump to conclusions. Let people have their say, let them say their side of the story.

Work if you can. Don't stress yourself out, over matters which

are out of your hands. Write. Read.
Luisteren. Talk, type.

That's all for today. Take it easy.

24 : JoJo's Confession

Back to the interrogation process :
"So, JoJo, if you mind me calling
you that. Tell me some more about
your crimes…"
　　　No comment

"Is it true that you killed someone?
Did someone over?
Acted inappropriately?
You know the longer you hold out,
the worse it will be for you?
The longer you hold out, the worse
it will get!?"

"Listen copper, I am not no snitch. And even if I did admit those crimes, I can barely remember any of them.

I've got assets now, and I'm not just talking about my bank balance"

"So, you wrecked the economy in two thousand and seven, and then again in two thousand and eight, both times when you fled to Africa, to seek the comfort in a love, you eventually realized? Is that it? Is that all you have to say for yourself?"

"Like I said, *bro*, you can't blame me for fleeing the UK My natural birthplace may be Manchester. But my original origin, the home of all of mankind is Eden. Read it on a

map. The home of Adam and Eve.
Eden East Africa Kenya!

God is our ultimate price, we all
have to pay. And that's if you can
even see him through the glow!?

"So, you think that you can make it
to heaven, after what you've done.
I doubt it. I doubt that very much!"
     "Well officer, fortunately, it
isn't down to you to decide my
fate. This is a topic I have given
some consideration. Because I
believe, that just as the youth hold
our future, so too does God hold
our dominion. And if he has
mercy, and a heart, which I
sincerely believe he does, then how
could an all-powerful, and omni
present entity, allow the puny
mortals of this life, face eternal

171

damnation in the next? How could he?

I will tell you how... He couldn't. I'm not saying I don't believe in Hell. Sure, I do. But this whole, burn for eternity in damnation, sounds a bit too much old testament to me...

Because like I said, you can be saved. Sinners can repent. In this life, and maybe even in the next.

Jesus? Man. Son of God sure, but more than that, he was the son of man. He says this repeatedly in the Bible. His name is Jesus Christ, he is the son of man. Baptized by John. And they both paid the ultimate price. So was John's penalty for helping the Jews, and lighter than Jesus'. Is having your head removed from your

shoulder's any easier way to go,
than a crucifixion?

Or to be hung, go ask
Saddam Hussein, about that one…
The ultimate general, the ultimate
war. Prove your manhood, by
taking it out on a defenceless
enemy. And look at the aftermath.

I've just offended Christians,
Veterans, and others as well.
But I've been honest. And So, help
me Lord, if that's one thing I am
good at that is my honesty.

I was even considering
telling my consultant, when I next
see him, of my crimes. I think I
need to, just to get them off my
chest. God help me, it will provide
him with ammunition for my
downfall.

Hopefully he won't do this, and I just pray that when I die, my name doesn't hit the press, in the worst possible way. Like it has for several creepy celebrities in recent years!

But for all the good people I have known in this life. Those who have known me at my best, and at my worst. Well I hope I have touched enough hearts, to leave space for one more in his almighty kingdom.

I do believe in multiple dimensions. My illness, at first a curse. But hold with it long enough, and it opens new doors, never imagined.

Like when I punched my dad smack bang in the face. Or shot him in the arm with an air rifle.

But then, I remember when he called all the doctors to his house, to carry out an emergency mental health act assessment, and have me committed for two years. Hell, that was tough. I'd say, along, with hitting the point three on the seven point scale of life signs, in my induced coma (which basically means I died), and sleeping rough for a few nights, and facing eternity in oblivion, when I faced divorce, or struggling with the mess of a five year degree, which I swear to god was another challenge. Or going through Primary and Secondary schools, without making any friends. Damn I've seen a lot.

So, what now? You want me to plead guilty?

Damn you. Damn you man. I will stand true to my God, my wife, and her children. That is what I am talking about. I will support them in their future and support every single man who has ever lost a loved one, and child, who has had to learn to survive on her own two feet. Or baby, that has leaned to speak, crawl, walk and smile.

We don't just live in this world. Our presence and being can be felt far above and below!"

25

Okay JoJo my brother. How about if I take you down a long journey. A journey with fifteen years behind you, and a good fifteen ahead. At least. A journey which has seen the back of more than one good man (I'm thinking scruffy Nick and Roy the landlord here), and multiple entrances into the mental health system, with few outs. It's like a game of poker (" All in"). Or chess (" check, checkmate") And so on. And so, you see, there is no one way to do this.

Retain control of your sanity. Stay in touch with your family. Make good friends. Drop the bad ones. There have been times when I have needed such friends in my life, when I had no one and I was desperate to cling on to anyone I could. Then I sought friendship with some real nasty pieces of work. Including a kid ten years my junior, who robbed me blind, and one ten years my senior, who persuaded to me that he had seen online videos of my wife, which led to me ripping up my marriage certificate. Scumbags both.

Anyway, what were we saying? Oh yes, use your truths to pronounce your story, as it appears to your mind. There is no one right or wrong way of writing your book. Thousands, hell millions have died in countless wars, from World War Two, to Vietnam, to Iraq, to give us the ability to speak our minds and truths, to you the reader, in this way!

We are built to fall in love with one person. Yet in times of passion, and loneliness, it is easy to forget this fact. Try to remember. Put the days of forgetfulness behind you. We live in a universe of parallel dimensions. Or space time warps, or coloured reflections,

and shimmering forcefields. Or
Terabytes, and nano drops. Of new
friendships with old acquaintances,
and old memories with new
friends.

Time is not fixed. Victory is
determined by the winners, sure.
Yet he who is left standing, can
always have their voice heard.
Liars will lie. Are you ever a liar?
Have you ever lied? Do you
always tell the truth? I doubt it.
And if it is to protect the meek and
wards? Well more bravo you.

That responsibility which
starts with our loins, walks with us
down the aisle, on through
graduation, and on to our death
bed. Life is a not a right it's a
privilege. Don't count your
blessings when it's too late.

Say thanks every day. Thank
you for the food on your plate, and
the company you keep. Respect his
knowledge and her body. Spend
time with your friends. You never
know when you might need them.
One day, they will be taken away
from us. All of them, one by one.
So, hold on to what is good, whilst
you still can.

JoJo out.

26 : What We Can Do for You?

"So, the next question JoJo is what
can we do for you?"

"Restart contact with my wife and child?

Provide a regular income, with a bank balance remaining, to give to my loved ones, if I die?

Not beat me up, knock me out, or mean that I must go hungry, ever again…

To provide food on my table, music on my stereo, books on my bookcase, and games on my forty-inch television?"

"Done done. Is there anything else good sir, before we call this meeting to a close?"

"Yes. I want you to give me friends. Friends, in high places, as well as on the streets.

I want you to give me a family. I want you to give me a degree. I want you to make me a fluid and experienced writer, who people will *want* to read? Not just because they know me!

I want you to take me to conferences in the capital. And make the women who I like to look and stare at, look and stare back at me.

I want you to heal my breathing, the indomitable wheeze, that happens every time I struggle for breath. Stop that.

I want you to make people want to talk to me, rather than just reply out of courtesy. I want you to repair the damage of the social rift, that has happened in my family. Largely my own doing. But I want you to help me heal this, as I indeed am making a conscious choice, to get on better with them myself.To tell me to *stop* when I go too far?!

I want you to make me a
chess grandmaster, so that I can
play players of a much better
rating, say eighteen/nineteen
hundred plus and beat them. I
want you to make me capable to
losing to beginners. Which is a skill
that not many chess *experts*, are
capable of.

I want you to give me
enough money to continue to give
my child pocket money and buy
my family meals to celebrate our
memorable days.

I want you give me a capital
platform, which continues to gain
quarter after quarter. I want you to
reduce my medications, and help
my medical consultant psychiatrist,
to see what it is like to live in my
shoes, as well as do the pre-

emptive risk prevention, on my yearly consultations with him?

I want you to help my wife stay in love with me, and fall in love with me again, if she has fallen out of it?

I want you to improve my acting skills. Characterization, improvisation, and vocalization.

I want you to make me a good person. I want you to heal the wounds of those I have hurt, and rebuild the lives, of those I have destroyed.

I want you to give my nurses and consultants, understanding, and cooperative patients.

I want you to help the cultures and communities I live in, heal, and grow. I want you to bless firstly this world, and dimension, and then the multi-verse and other planets, with love, and understanding and temperance.

I want you to heal the wounds of war and mend the trauma of death.

I want to live, and finally I want to die?"

"We'll see what we can do," the man in the police uniform uniform replied!

27 : Friends

I never really had any friends at school. Sure, I got my first taste of reading, from these studies. And I chatted to some girls in my final year. Even had a girlfriend. But you know, I was kind of a disturbed kid.

Then when I got run over in 1997, gave me a broken neck and serious head injury. Led to a coma, one I have never fully come out of.

I like writing, because here I can return to the world of dreams. In my head and on page, for you our dear readers to share.

Anyway, like I said, I never really had any friends at school. Not at primary school, not at secondary school. Then at college, I made my first friend. A cute girl, who I went later to marry. And she has given me a beautiful stepdaughter.

My sister on the other hand, had loads of friends at primary school, loads at secondary school, and she also met her now husband at university. I used to wonder how she did it.

In the years between me leaving school and getting kicked out from my mum's house at Nineteen, I first made some friends (from my own peer group). And do you want to know how I did it? Well it was by playing online chess, on the computer, on the internet, before the whole 'internet' thing really kicked off...
If I remember correctly, the first two chess applet's (programs), I remember playing were 'Excite' and 'Yahoo' chess. Excite eventually changing hands to 'Pogo' before it became obsolete and disbanded altogether. I remember spending many a glorious hour, on the computer,

trying out various openings, and
becoming good at a few of them.

It is a shame really what has
happened to online chess
nowadays, seeing as computer
aided players, although officially
refused (like it the server's catch
you using an engine to find the
'correct' moves, you *will* be
banned), but still people use them.
More now than ever before.
This explains why we will come
across players of pitiful rankings,
who will come up with the perfect
moves to beat us, time after time.
Or almost every time. I know I
have already done a chapter on
chess, so I won't dwell on this for
too long. So, the best we can do to
counter this is to adopt 'anti'
computer chess tactics. Playing out
of the opening book's moves and

forcing the struggle of minds to come to the fore. We may come worse off, but at least we will give them a run for their money. Because I tend to find these players who use computer lines, or deeply memorized openings, may flounder and panic when forced into a tactically open middle and end games.

I remember a game I played recently where I kept the enemy on his toes, and then near the end of the game I made an oversight, which left my Queen hanging/exposed, but he didn't see it and retreated instead. Which let me then close in for the win. That felt good.

I do like playing online chess and making friends on here that way. Even if these are people, you will never meet in person, most likely never meet again. It is still a good way to interact. And here on safe spaces on the internet, there is a whole world of geeks, nerds, intellects, and as I said already, cheats, who share the odd half an hour, putting the outside world away, and joining in the battle of sixteen versus sixteen pieces, over a battle terrain of sixty four checked squares. I am very fond of this game. And as I just said, I have made many good friends this way. If you can count digital encounters, as friends?

As for real friends, the flesh and blood variety… It wasn't really until my numerous admissions to hospital from 1997 through to December 2018 (all with psychotic/schizophrenic symptoms), that I changed from a loner without friends, to a popular team player. So, these days, I always have a friend or two I can call on my mobile. And that isn't my dad. Lol.

I feel a bit sorry for our elder generations, who seem to still be struggling to master these new technologies. And compared to our youths, who have grown up with them. It's like the internet.

Yes, I know I have been banned form nearly all the martial arts forums out there, and a good deal more as well. As I have to some extent explored in some of my other books (especially *A Patient in Time*). I mean these days I have been lucky enough to find a small, but decent forum to post in, called (***), who the likes of *** (the

owner), and ***, have kept me out
of trouble for the past few years. At
least I have been able to share some
of my life's woes on here, and not
be banned.

It is like even at University, I
still had a lecturer or three, who
seemed to have it in for me. But
let's forget about them.

And instead hold on to the
great notion of learning and self-
improvement, that these
institutions hold for us. I must
agree, even if I may have struggled
to at the time, that these were truly
formative years of my life. Not to
mention, that my studies kept me
out of hospital.

So, friends. Yes study, work
hard. But also play hard. Make
friends, talk to others. It doesn't
matter if you are the most popular

person in your class, or one of the loners. Carry on your work. And have faith. Because God loves you. Remember, everyone matures at different rates. And as you do get more mature, and find your niche in this life, so to the dark clouds of our past, will make way for the sunny skies, of our future.
I truly believe in this notion of progress, and hope. And hopefully if you bear with me you can too!

28 : Money

Okay here we go : Money, we all know what that is right? The green you get on pay day, right?
Wrong. I learned a lot of things at my time at university. Not really

stuff I was taught, more stuff I picked up myself, along the way. One of which being that money, or wealth, is only what you make of it.

So, what are you most valuable assets? Your house? Your car? Your sky television subscription?

How about your friends, your family, your career, your education?

So, my money? Well for want of betraying confidentiality, it's all these things.

My expertise in surviving the mental health system. Its sure cost me a lot these fifteen years I've been locked away, and on heavy medications. But hell, it must have cost the National Health Service a comparable fortune, to do this to me?

Then I think it is in all our interests, to keep me well, and out of hospital. And that doesn't always equate to heavy dose of medication. Although, it sadly, seems like it *does*, sometimes...

What else? Back to the realm of money. Despite not actually making much, I am sitting on a healthy trust fund, which protects my portfolio from the Department for Work and Pensions, challenges. It was a hell of a six-month challenge, to get them to let me keep this. But I provided the legal framework/ruling, which in the end they had to comply with. And back to my family. I see my role in this life, now, as that of a protector. I am here to look after my wife, and her children. To support them, not just with money, but with *time and love*.

The exact things, I'm not able to provide, from secure hospital settings. So, there you go.

In this life, we don't always have it easy. And whilst faith in God, does help. Sometimes, you need to commit to a hand. And put your chips in investments, that others won't always be able to see, let alone understand.

But trust your own strategies. Make friends. Fight your enemies. Try to avoid breaking the law. But most of all, do what is right.

Whilst God is our ultimate saviour, and judge. So too, we need to live in this life, with the consequences of our actions, and

the knowledge that our legacies
will hopefully be around for a long
time, after our blood and cells,
have returned to the mother Earth,
from whence we came.

And hopefully our spirits
and souls, can return blessed to
their makers.

29 : Gaming Dreams

"So, what did you do today JoJo?"
Today I played on my console. An
Xbox One X.
I played with my daughter. Black
Ops three. Firstly, we played
zombies. And fought off hordes
and hordes of the undead. Firstly,
buying a nice shooting handgun,
then roaming the city, trying to
have the other's back, and wiping

out these undead, until, eventually
every time, they became too much
for us, and overwhelmed our
limited firepower. Especially when
our ammo ran out, and we couldn't
find the ammo dumps.

"And after that?"
After that I introduced her to a
new, bonus, game mode I recently
discovered. Free running. There is
a total of four courses, and I have
completed the first three. The first
one, for beginners, is quite nice and
simple. A quick jump, or boosted
jump, some swimming, fast
paddle. The odd target, one of
which must be taken on the move,
and a couple of wall jumps.

Now these are a little bit
tricky at first. And I'll be damned if
I haven't got cramp from
struggling to master this

manoeuvre. It isn't so hard when you only must jump onto a single wall, run along it, and then jump off. Or even from one wall, on to a second.

But when there are multiple walls, then it gets trickier. The real challenge for me today, was something I did before I saw my kid. This was when I tried the third level, which is for experts. And there are a couple of buildings, where starting at the bottom, you must free run up a box structure building with no easy paths. Literally overcoming gravity, and having to build curves into your trajectory, so the right-angle walls, don't stop your momentum. This was tricky. Given the penalties I had to endure for all the restarts I did, I think my record for this level, is something like forty-five minutes. Yes, it really was that hard. And my hand has been in tremor, after all the cramp I have been giving it.

But you know, when, and if I play these free runs again, tomorrow, my hand will be stronger, and better equipped to deal with this brutality.

I realize this may well not seem to relate to martial arts. At least not on appraisal. But don't forget that hand movement and control, is crucial for all the martial arts. At least it is for the four I know best : Kung Fu, Aikido, Judo and Karate. So, the ability to grip, control, project, and counter (reverse), are all hand movements. And with a stronger hand, a more flexible and in control five digits, my martial arts, should, and will, improve alongside.

Not to mention this team playing, with my kid is building a foundation, balancing on the digital world, but aiming at the stars. One day I will be gone. And I can only hope that my daughter is able to share with her children the knowledge and companionship, that we have built together.

30 : Signs of the Zodiac

Control, discipline, friends, family, and love.
We need all these things.
Life is sometimes like a whirlpool, a whirlwind.

Stumbling from step to step, from hold to hold. Out of options, out of gas, out of control.

And where do we end? Where we left off? Or in a different place, a different space. A new galaxy, remedy, or fortune. If you read the stars, I'm a Pieces. Or by the Chinese zodiac, a Rooster.

I suffer from insomnia. Or maybe sometimes I just forget to go to sleep. My dad blames me for this. But I blame the medications. I have had this problem, right the way through my university life. And boy was I kicking myself when I missed out on a first for my university undergraduate dissertation. But on review, I realized that it had spelling mistakes halfway through the

document. And you must
appreciate that any spelling
mistakes, even one, will prevent
this sacrosanct document from
ever reaching that pinnacle grade.
Which is a shame really. Seeing as I
did over a hundred different
versions, in preparation.

Later I read that a Bachelor's
degree isn't supposed to create *new*
knowledge, only better present
what's already out there. But I will
be damned if I didn't do that and
more.

At least I have now paved
the way for my daughter and wife,
to reach this qualification, if they
so choose. A degree, is only as
good as the people taking it?
Wrong, only as good as the
lecturers? To some extent. Maybe

only as good as the effort you put
in.

Do I regret doing one? Not
on your life. I learned so much.
About African drama, and
education, and sociology, and in
my research about mental health.
For example, you may have known
that during the holocaust, Hitler
rounded up the mentally ill, and
send them to the extermination
camps? But what you probably
didn't know is that across Europe,
Britain, and even America, there
were also programs to Euthanize,
sterilize and otherwise deal with
the problem patients. The
psychiatrists labelled then
Dementia Praecox. Now more
commonly known as
schizophrenia.

So, what else? I did some more gaming today. Reached a couple of new record times for the beginner and advanced Call of duty, Black Ops Three free run courses. This gives me cramp in my left hand, when I play it for too long. Mainly as a result of over pressure on the back of the hand, from having to press down on the left joystick, at the same time as moving to stick, and pressing the buttons with the other hand.

Now the day after, I can play it again, hit the new records, and pull off the moves I was struggling to achieve yesterday, with some ease. I am looking forward to playing on it again with my kid, to impress her with these results. Also, I want to teach her how to wall run up the inside of the buildings, in the penultimate level, which is hard, but there is a trick to it.

What is needed for you to jump at quarter turn angles, with quick succession, to mount the beast. Ride the tiger. If you will excuse my colourful language? Thank God.

Nog iets anders?
No that will do for now. Bear with me. Peace out.

31 : Sharing

When we write, we do so to share with others… It may be a cathartic (healing) process. It may help us to unravel some of the tied-up feelings and tensions, the long day's the past has brought to our shoulders. But all together, it is not only for our eyes to peruse. We write, primarily perhaps, to share these deep harboured secrets with the world.

Some books become best sellers. Others only remain but the domain of the elite few. But the process of writing, and primarily reading (which is, after all, at the heart of every good writer's foundation), is one of sharing. One of therapy. One of memories (*souvenirs* in French). One of times, places, people and moments, locations, facts, and fiction. Writing is, to me, a case of casting the living dynamic world, to a side for one moment. And digging back into that gold mine of your mind, the *good times*. The powerful people we have met, and the memorable moments we have gathered from them.

It is static. It is frozen, forever, on the white paper page of the publication. Whether we have self-published or managed to source a professional to do the job with us.

People, children, our future, our elders and the dead Rest in Peace, the times who have passed before us. And our peers, all battling it out for a slice of the cherry. And does it matter if we win? Does it matter if we become best sellers? What if we discover a new truth in reading? A new sense of competence, a new joy in finding other authors. To share, to explore, to learn from.
There is so much more, to the world, than meets the uniform eye.

And as we learn, we learn that we will always be learning. Or at least, that that is the goal.

One of the beautiful things about doing my Joint Honours Degree, was that rather than just being stuck in the realm of Sociological insight, I also got to learn about Theatrical, (both Shakespeare, and African dramatic) truths. Which at an undergraduate level, is quite impressive? So, for the Shakespeare third year unit, it was standard, for us to be reading a play a week. And then extra backup reading and watching materials as well. It was standard for me to spend many the lunch hour, or late into the afternoons, locked away in the library, head deep in books, or in films. And this was great.

And for the African dramas, discovering new texts, new ways of acting, and researching these, and even finding for example in one of the plays my grandfather Robbie, was mentioned... Everything seemed to be falling in to place. And so, what I only ever got a two : two (C) grade for these modules. In fact I was over the moon to hit these targets, seeing as my class mates were mostly academic young women, many of which had come straight from sixth form education, and were already brimming with the correct academic rigor, to ace these grades. So, like I was saying, up against these star peers, my grades take a new shine.

And so, what if there were at
least two (again female) lecturers
who clearly had it in for me?
Women, who in age terms were
my juniors, and gave very little in
terms of content, to be taught, in
their lectures. And then had the
audacity to mark me down, on my
essays. Putting ceiling grades of Ds
(thirds, or 40%), at the end of these
semesters! And you know the way
I have learned to research above
and beyond the scope of my lesson
plans, to find out new ideas and
schema, new mod ii, and creations,
to adorn my work with. For the
presentations, and then bringing
these back down to Earth, for
classroom, and power-point
consumption. Well that went to
shoot when I had these time
wasters.

It was like, they had lived their whole lives, being at the top of the class, learning their ways. And when somebody stepped out of the folds, and did it a different way, well clearly this was no good for them.

You know the turnover of lecturers across my five-year degree, was quite high. Like a lot. So, to be honest with you, there were only a couple of lecturing staff on my lesson roster, who kept with us from the start. And I've seen at least five, maybe more, lecturers leave, either to better universities (one to Scotland and one to Sheffield), one of my lecturers left to go to Vietnam, to hook up with an old flame, which I don't think lasted, one got the sack because his mathematical statistics,

were not taken kindly to by the
softer humanitarian approach
favoured by my Sociological class
mates, and one simply left the
undergraduate teaching pool to
help out with building the multi-
faith centre, although it appears he
has now moved on from this as
well.

Then this in turn, was then
outdone by the number of students
who dropped out. I remember one
mature student, who was so
disgusted by one of the *bad*
lecturers, I have already
mentioned, that she either felt
unable, or was failed by this
reader, so that she was *academically*
unable, like it was *impossible*, for her
to get a passing grade. Which is
quite disgusting really? That in this
day and age, a university which

considers itself to be pretty good, to be employing these people in the first place. This student was a mature student like me, and I remember spending time talking to her, and at that point it was looking doubtful that either of us were going to finish the degree with a pass, let alone honours grade!? I persevered, but I didn't see her on graduation.

Both lecturers I have here mentioned, have stories behind them, which I could ruminate over, but for the sake of anonymity, and to stave of future libel actions, I'm not going to cough up. It is quite disgusting that people like this, who would fail my classmates, because they didn't conform to their mentality, or whatever reason it was they used to do this. Moving swiftly on.

Back to the theme at hand : *Sharing*. It's something that parents do with each other when they make their children. Something that kids do with their mum and dads, when they discuss how their school days had been.

Something that friends do with each other, when they play football in the park or the yard, or play chess or draughts over the checked board, or cards over the table.

Actors do on stage, or for television or the movies. Something that politicians do with their peers, their party, their houses, or representatives, parliament, the lords, or the senate Not to mention, and perhaps most importantly, the public. Both nationally and for the broader global image. They do it to share!?

History is written, and to some extent drafted, by the winners. But it is the people at the bottom, the people sweeping up, the people watching the ten year plus DVD replays, who outnumber these winners by ten thousand to one. And it are these second-rate citizens, our voice, that is just as important as the ruby wielding 'winners' at the top of the spectrum.

They can all go to hell as far as I am concerned!

32 : Bhangra Dancing

Tonight, I danced to Bhangra music, using Kung Fu moves,

which I have creatively Christened
Dance Fu! It's something which I
used to do quite a lot, at my old
address. It lets you try out new
moves, whilst developing a good
sense of rhythm, and bodily
coordination.

I also used two of my
favourite Chi Gong moves (similar
to Tai Chi, but more closely related
to Kung Fu), the first called 'lifting
the sky', where standing, you
throw your arms out to the side,
then lift them up to the top, to
connect before bringing them back
down in equilibrium, to your
centre. And I even extended this to
touching my toes a few times
(which I barely managed, as I am
quite out of shape).

Then the second move is
called 'Pushing Mountains', where

you basically lift both hands,
parallel to your chest, then extent
them outward in front of your, like
you are doing press ups in the air. I
did these for a song or two as well.
These also build internal strength. I
didn't do any push ups today. I
will save that for another time.

  After dancing for seventeen
of the songs, I was exhausted. I
also did some drunken master
monkey dancing, which is basically
where you sway from side to side,
and throw punches, both closed
fist and open handed, as well as
giving away the back of your hand,
and giving away the palm (which
in a real life situation can be
converted to a grab, or a throw),
and countless Ikkyos, which is the
first pin in Aikido. And the only
move I can say I am good at. But

it's also the first move the police, and security services, use to take down the perpetrators of crime, so it is handy to have in your arsenal.

33 : A Rest in Peace

I remember one of the first times I was arrested, about the turn of the millennium. I had been shown Ikkyo by my auntie's then boyfriend, who was a strong black man called Danny. And he showed me this move. At the time I couldn't remember it, but I have since then been trained in how to do an expert Ikkyo, from firstly Karate classes, then I got it down to a tee with Aikido, which I hold a Yellow belt in.

Danny was a high ranking black belt in Karate, Dan grade material. And whilst after learning this move in two or three demonstrations, in my mum's old front room, I did understand one thing he showed me, which is the first point of this move. Which is to say that that the thumb is the weak point of the grip. For whilst we may have five other non-thumb digits on each hand, we only have one thumb. Consequently, when someone grabs you, it is easier to knock the hand off, using your opposite arm/hand. In a strike to the offending hand, in a forty-five-degree angle to the opposing grip. This releases the grip.

And so, one day, after giving the one finger salute to a police patrol car, then proceeding to

being chased away by an irate
officer. I didn't get very far before
he caught up with me. But imagine
the shock on his face, when he
grabbed me with his big, manly
hand, and I simply knocked it off,
with the ease of someone who
evidently knew what they were
doing. Which seeing as this was
the first time, I had used this move,
I didn't. But it didn't work, so yes,
thanks Danny. Thanks Karate.
Ikkyo, which is basically an
extension, a fruition, a maturation
of this move. Which says, hey, why
not rather than just remove his
grip, keep it in place, and rotate
your body round, again in a forty-
five-degree angle oblique to the
offender, to bring him down to the
ground?

Then some years later, me and Joey, another one of my mentally unstable friends, got in a fight in a city centre cafe. Well I say got in a fight, I attacked him truth be told. But this guy is always such on edge, he really did have it coming to him. Sorry, no, I didn't do Ikkyo, I did another one of my repertoires of killer martial arts moves. The "headlock", which brought him crashing down over the tables and patrons, all of whom tried to look away, as I punished him. Okay, this is graphic language, and Joey was, and always will be a mate. But he did tell me that it messed him up for a good while afterward. Anyway, we made up.

And you know even the headlock, which is a powerful move, when used correctly, has a development, maturation, which goes from nasty, to killer. Which is reverse Guillotine. Which is effective on the floor in groundwork, Judo randori for example. But a killer when used on the street, on an unsuspecting perpetrator.

Which is exactly what I did do, a while after the scrap with Joey. Some homeless punk once saw me walking to my local gym, which is in the city centre, and saw my large purse, protruding from my jacket, nabbed it, and ran away from me (legged it). Well not wanting my martial art's training to fail me, I chased him up the street, and put him down using this very move. The reverse Guillotine. He was so shocked at this move, plus it attacks the spine near the base of the neck, so caused a temporary black out. In this time, I retrieved my Chinese medicine balls, which he had also nabbed, but forgot to pick up my purse/wallet. So, then I waited for a bit, in which time, he revived, saw that my purse was still there for the plucking, picked it up and ran off. I was later able to reclaim the money taken out from my wireless credit cards, because they are insured. So, this is the second move I was able to use effectively on an unsuspecting opponent.

34 : Other ideas

Do I know any other martial arts moves? A few. Break-falling, which I learned at Judo as a kid, and then again at Aikido. Whilst the break-fall necessarily interrupts the collision of your body, when after being thrown/taken down, with the slap of your arm/hand. Because it is better to let a limb take the shock of this collision, than suffering the damage to the torso/midriff/centre.

I'm not going to slag off my martial arts teachers. Because we need to respect our elders. But I have my own way, and my own learnings, which much like doing the degree, are something, a way if you will, which I have now honed, and refined. And cannot be taken away from me, just because they don't mar with their learned ways. Please read my second and third books, A *Patient in Time : JoJutsu* and *Fighting Madness* both available at Amazon and all good bookstores, if you want further insight into the genesis, engagement, development, and fruition of my martial art. In that book I called it JoJutsu, not to be confused with the staff fighting discipline which shares the same name. But instead, an ontology rooted in the central character of many of my stories. Jo. Or as in here, to use his full name JoJo. Good luck!

35 : Life's Challenges

In this life we are faced with challenges. From emerging from the womb, to learning to crawl, walk, speak, and read.

We struggle through school, college, and university. Struggle to hold down a job. Keep hold of a loved one. And then watch as your child goes through the same traumas we did.

Only we hope that their lives are easier than ours were. We want them to climb and soar, where we stumbled and fell.

So is it easy? Sometimes. Sometimes it is incredibly hard. There is a wide range of literature available today, from both online stores (notably Amazon and eBay), the brick and mortar bookshops (Waterstones springs to mind), and now in the digital age even Kindle and Google books, vie for position in this ever evolving world.

But whilst some people may like to sit down with an eBook, I much prefer a paper, or hard back edition. I say we must prepare our children for the world, to give them opportunities so they don't suffer like we did. But the sharpest swords, are forged in the hottest fires. And we can't molly coddle our children for all their lives in case they never grow up.

It's like me learning how to cook. I first learned in home economics lessons, at secondary school. Which were good. These helped. That is where I first learned to make my legendary rock buns.

But over the years, especially living by myself, I have picked up some good skills such, as gaging how hot an oven, or plate, is needed, before putting the food in/on.

Some people have only ever cooked by the book. So, if you ask them to cook a staple food, pasta for example, without a timer, they will struggle.

Or like being a vegetarian. It was always a lifelong dream of mine, to stop eating meat once and for all. Which seems to be a target I have been doing quite well at sticking to, for the past couple of years or so.

When I was in hospital, I sometimes ate meat. I mean there is such a limited range on the menu, it was out of sheer desperation if anything. A cry for help.
But would I recommend their meat? No sorry. With pork, beef, and fish, that don't reassemble anything known to man. Perhaps I am being mean. But the meat wasn't great!

36 : A letter to the powers that be

I'm kind of like a prisoner of war.
In two thousand and three I
opposed the invasion of Iraq, and
subsequent capture and execution
of Saddam, I have been arrested
and sectioned, more times since,
than beggar's belief. I distinctly
remember being kept in the ward
at the Kingsway intensive care unit
PQ, with an air-light, for the
burning summer of 2007. That was
difficult. We nearly cooked alive!

Also, all my crimes, up to
two thousand and seventeen were,
(except for me smashing up the
Ford Escort car in 2005), were
committed on a ward, when I was

on medication. I know you have a responsibility to the public, to keep them safe from me. And I have tried to work closely with my social care team, mum, dad, sister, wife, consultant, and community treatment manager.

This road has taken a long time. And I'm thirty-nine now, so I'm not getting any younger. My wife has been a godsend and blessing, and she continues to meet me. I want to stay well so that I can continue to see them. Even my last doctor agrees how much better I am on this new medication.

I don't know what your criteria are for me coming off them, or at least having the medications reduced are? Hopefully you can see for yourself the progress I have made. I have also switched from

cigarettes to vaping about six
months ago. Today my dad
suggested waiting two years,
before any reduction takes place.
And if you are happy with this, I
am prepared to concur. Up to you?
J

37 : Respite

Sleep. That most beautiful of
things, when you lay down on
your pillow, and let the world of
troubles wash over your head. You
close your eyes and return to the
land of dreams. Where the troubles
of your life, wash away. And the
angels of your life, return to the
playing field.

    I suffer from insomnia. That
is where, I struggle to sleep at a

decent time. Often find me awake for twenty-four, thirty-six, or even longer periods of time. I find myself reassembling a vampire, zombie, or werewolf in that respect.

Sometimes, I log in to my games at night. Be it Call of Duty, Lichess, or Dominance Poker. Sometimes I do cook, sometimes (quite frequently) listening to music. A range of activities, to keep myself occupied at night.

I once imagined myself to be an old general. Navigating the battlefields, on my horse, like Napoleon, or Wellington. And commanding my armies, to fight off the hordes of trolls, zombies, and demons, that would affront us daily. And there were times when I was knocked off my horse, and again like Napoleon, taken captive on an island, to serve my time. This is how I felt, every time I was captured, by the mental health services. A prisoner, a prisoner of war.

And rather than just comply, I would fight them. From expressing my individuality, and with kisses, to asking them not to give me the iron tablets, or antibiotics. Which always seemed to mess with my internal constitution.

I don't like taking drugs. And fair play to them, they know as well as I do, that I am hoping for the day, when I can come off them all together.

I have been on anti-psychotic medications, of one sort or another, for the best part of fifteen years.

Over which course, I have had over a dozen hospital admissions, in and out, generally lasting Seven months. But the last time I went in, it was for two years. Both here in Derby, and over to Bradford, for a sixth month stint. Boy that was a killer. Imagine going from a thirty a day smoking habit, to none. This was tough. And for all these prisons and hospitals, which have banned smoking completely, fair play to them. God knows how they do it.

Then I would get two a day, then four, finally six, eight, and I think eventually I was let back home to Derby.

I met Michael Jackson in hospital. Or at least I thought it was him? It may not have been, but he did a Jackson style twirl, and I

have never known anyone else
who could do this? He told me
how upset he had been when the
social services took his kids off
him. That is further evidence. And
he taught me the importance of
knees and elbows, in a street fight!
This was good practical advice,
which may one day save my life?!
He got out before me; I hope he is
okay.

I also met a guy who I called
Vietnam child. He reminded me a
son I might have had with Min, my
Chinese 'friend', I met at a charity
shop some years earlier. I never
slept with her, only cuddled her on
a couple/few occasions. And I'm
not sure if you can make a baby,
that way. Anyway …

So yes, I was able to connect Vietnam kid, with his family, on the pay phone. Who were eventually able to visit, and then rescue him, from this trap?

I also met an atheist friend, from Afghanistan, I think. He didn't really speak much English, if any. But I was able to communicate with him, by a combination of sign and body language. I also thought he was blind, by the way he seemed to stare. I even on a couple of occasions, closed my eyes, and tried to navigate the small area which consisted of the ward, by touch and memory alone. This was difficult, but gives me some good insight into the perils, and hardship, blind people face. The things we do when we are mad!

And finally, there were a good number of admirable staff members here. Probably the most famous one, was Alex Ferguson, who had retired from football, to become a senior carer, at this mental health unit. He was a good guy. And I was sad to find out he died, a few years later. At least that was what I heard?

There were also a couple of staff members who I don't think they were an item, although they might have been. Anyway, they had both served as royal officers, in the armed or naval services. And I was impressed by their courage, and steadfast determination, to look after their wards, and help us all get better.

There were a lot of other people on this unit as well. Hell, I have met a lot of people over the years, some of my best friends, have been made in hospital. And I have known a lot of good staff workers as well. I tip my hat to them I really do.

Okay boys and girls, I think that is about enough on this topic, of sleep, and hospital. I hope I will never have to go in again, but statistically I would say the odds are against me. At least now, I have a stable home life, with regular visits from my family, and a close connection to my carers, as well as other friends, I talk to, and see on a regular basis. Take good care, and sweet dreams.

38 : Health

Control. Respect. Love.

Remember the good times. Think about them. Remember the friends you have made along the way, new ones too. Focus on them.
People you have met, conversations you have had. Places you have been to. Good music, that you have listened to.

This life isn't a short one. You have lived for a long time, and God willing you have a long time to go. Don't rush into things. But if you do, embrace them. Hold on to what's good. Read, play, eat, sleep. I wish I could sleep. It's like back in '97 I went into a coma, one which I've still not fully woken up from. Glimpse your medical infirmities and try your best *despite* these.

Spend your money wisely, when you have it. And when you don't, save.

How many times do I have to say this to you? You are beautiful. And it doesn't matter who you are, or what you are feeling right now. Every man and woman, who has ever loved, was once a baby. The greatest pinnacle of humanity. Remember this. Hold on to this hope. And no matter your position, whether you consider your life a success, or a failure at this point. There is still time to turn it around.

Take it from me, the man who once hit rock bottom. From a Primary and Secondary education. To get hit by a speeding car and face my first seven-month hospital admission. From losing my first and only true friend, when she left the country, and I thought I might never see her again. To being kicked out of my house and sleeping rough for a night.

The car accident, eventually some years later, won me a decent playout. But for over ten years after this, the money was locked away. And these so-called expert solicitors, did a damn fine job at spending it for me. Until there came the point, when it looked as if my money wouldn't even last me another five years, let alone the rest of my life.

And then there was my mental health problems. Something one of my consultant psychiatrist's, flattering called, *acute* and *chronic* Schizophrenia. Charming.

I have also been told by several medical professionals, that this is a lifelong condition, which I will have to take medication for, for the rest of my life? Am I happy with this? You better not believe it.

It is my good intentions to prove them all wrong!

You see I am on something called a community treatment order now, which is a section, they place on the most ill in the community. And at every review I have, which must be carried out by a doctor, a social worker, and a lay person, I think... Well I always present my best self, for coming off it. But at every review, at every tribunal I've ever had, they always reach the same decision. That it is better for me to stay on the CTO, rather than come off it. This is to starve off the risk of noncompliance with medicine, and medical treatment. Bull basically.

So, what else? My dad thinks he
knows me. He thinks he has read
my books, and supported me
through it? But was he there when
I got hit by a car? Was he there
when they attached electrodes to
my skull, and administered high
voltage electric currents? Was he
they when I asked my solicitors,
before the case was settled, to
accept a lower award, because I
was just frustrated at how long the
whole thing was taking, and
wanted to be done with it?
Was he there, when my wife won
the visa, in Nottingham
magistrates court (a big glass
building in Nottingham, near the
train station)? Was he there when I
had to settle the barrister's fee,
which came to many thousands?

Was he there, every time I got admitted? Was he on the ward with me, for every ward round, when I argued my silly socks off with the doctors, only to be told time and time again, that they *still* thought I was ill, and treatment? Time and time again!
Was he there when I got taken out of the court of protection?

I haven't been able to hold down a job for most of my working life, and all bar a few charity jobs and one brief stint at a nursing home, none. Be the crimes that I have committed will stay on my record. I seriously struggle at seeing me *ever* holding down, a nine to five job. It's okay…

I have been blessed to have met these two wonderful people. And every hour, every minute,

every second I spend with them,
being from the visits I get, or the
telephone contact, well this is all
when I am touched by heaven.

I will be sad when we must
leave each other, as death
separates, us all from our loved
ones, in the end. But I am hoping
to still have many more special
moments, and times, before that
day comes. But by then regret will
be too late. Let's hope that I can
make up for the bad karma I had as
a youth, with some positive energy
I have been able to kindle as a man.

39 : Recovery

Let us move on. I have magical
powers. Ask any of my friends,
and they will be able to confirm

this for you. The doctor says I don't have insight. But that is not true. I did a five-year degree, where every day I had to come to terms with my illness, to get the job done. And I only missed like one or two days over the whole five years, which was due to seasonal viruses. Where it would have jeopardized the safety of others, for me to go in. Anyway, back to the magic. Today, I turned the heating off in my lounge, and put it on in my bedroom, then went outside for a vape (I have stopped vaping in the house).

I have lived in my own house since the break of the year. Cooked my own food (cheesy pasta with mayonnaise and sauce), washed my own dishes, paid my own bills, and washed my own clothes. At the break of the year, I was also successful in winning my benefits, both full Universal Credit, and full Personal Independence payments. My once sweetheart left the country half the way though our college education, and never returned. At least that was how it seemed.

I finally managed to get her phone number, and hold the odd conversation with her, and write and receive the odd latter. But Still the future was looking bleak. Then finally in 2007 I was able to fly over to visit her. And she begun to make a man out of me. In 2008 we got married.

In 2012 I was able to visit again. This time doctor Tao told me the two conditions of me going, was that I took an injection dose over, to be administered over there. And that I took the anti-malaria tablets. Ever though I had had a severe reaction to them, the first time I took them. I took them prior to flying, and on the plane, but in Kenya I was so sick from a reaction to these tablets, that we agreed I wouldn't need to take them anymore.

This whole idea of me having no insight in to Schizophrenia is nonsense. I spent the whole of my final year at university studying it. From the black person's experience on locked wards, to the Nazi's final solution, and other varied, and complex ideas (see appendix). The final chapter in my essay, was on insight. And I have printed this off for you know. How the hell could I write a high-level piece of academic literature, on this subject, and not have at least a basic insight into the condition. It wouldn't be possible.

My community nurse and consultant have been using the same tripe lines "oh he's a risk to himself and others", "oh he would come of his medications if taken off a CTO". Tell me then, why for the seven years I was at university I persisted in taking them, even though halfway through when I was taken off the order (by mistake) I still took them at full dose?

I know you guys are so enamoured by these overpaid medics, I have had loads of tribunals before, and lost everyone. And it is always the same old arguments. Basically, it is me the little guy in the bottom, who must take it in the neck.

I'm not trying to deceive you. Unlike the *Doctors*, who change their stories every time, like a chameleon. I try to always tell the truth. Why the hell would I confess my sins, what possible good does that do me? Do you really think I just needed to get it off my chest? Idiots. No, I will tell you why I mentioned her, because I'm not afraid to tell the truth.

And the whole issue of magic, is kind of hard to explain. But my magical powers do increase, with the reduction of these medications. Sure, I want to come off them one day. But that day isn't today.

What I want today, is for you to remove this legal shackles, from around my neck, and also get an assurance from doctor Tao, or his successor, that they will agree to reduce my dose from the 405 mg it is at the moment (the maximum dose), to the 300 mg dose, which is the next step down.

I visit my nurse for the injection every month, without fail. This will continue. She has even offered to do extra meetings (to monitor my progress) if I do have this reduction. So, it's not as if there isn't a strong framework in place, to detect any sign of a relapse. I also have weekly visits by the community psychiatric nurse, and twice or thrice weekly visits by my support worker from Rethink.

Get off my back. Grow up, grow some, and leave me alone!

PS. Sorry for getting angry, but how would you feel if you had to spend the next fifteen years of your life, in and out of hospital, and under huge amounts of pressure over this time. That is the reason I want the CTO removing, to treat me like a human being, and not some subhuman, who can maintain a marriage, and home, and stepdaughter, and not be trusted to take my medication?

40 : Fight

Tonight, I got in a fight. Randori, sparring, call it what you want, with Will. It was the first one we have had in a while. And the same as the previous two, it ended in a draw.

It lasted two rounds. But whereas the first one saw me gassing out early, in this one I still gasses out in the first round, but I lasted the two, before we both agreed to call it quits. A draw.

But whilst I gassed out, he showed me his hands and he was shaking all over. I call that a psychological victory. And we could have gone on further, but like I said I didn't want to hurt him. I guess I need to start doing

some more pushups, to build my
anaerobic strength, and more long-
distance walks, to build my
cardiovascular strength.

There was a point when I
saw an opening for a kick, so I
threw a quick right front kick at his
leg. Only lightly, because as I said I
didn't want to hurt him. And then
he changed his guard to watch out
for my legs. We both went in with
some punches, and he is lucky that
I took my surrogate wedding ring
off, because my left jab would have
dominated him. I went to grab him
a few times, and he didn't try any
single arm grabs, but we did stand
still for a minute or so, just holding
on to each other.

I tried to apply pressure to
make him fall to the ground, but he

has good balance, and was able to resist this.

Then I got the front kick in, I already mentioned. I also saw an opening for a head butt, which would have done some serious damage to his face I'm sure. But like I have said, I didn't want to hurt him. Plus, I can save this move for the future, depending on what else happens.

I have also yet to use my trademark headlock, or reverse guillotine on him, which I have ended two separate fights within the past, with equal success. One against my mate Joey, who later told me I had him by surprise, and the other against a mugger in town, whom I was able to retrieve at least half of the booty he had stolen that day.

We even had a friend act as referee, and simultaneously film the fight on her phone. At least she said she filmed it. She also said that she would be uploading the video to Facebook, that night I thought. But she hasn't so far. Which makes me think that perhaps she didn't even film it in the first place. No matter. Another result for the angels. And the clouds where they live.

I think for the next fight, I am going to ask her to film it using my phone's video camera, so at least that way I will know that it has been recorded. And whilst it is true that the car park we squared off in, it was like midnight. So, all the neighbours were in bed. At least no one disturbed us. And like I said, we did have a ref.

But me and Will are good friends. He even said that he was just going to block my punches, although when the fight got started, we both got in some *Atemi* (strikes).

It's been over four years since I last did Aikido, and seven since I did it with a club that teaches the 'hard' way, so you might say I am a bit rusty. But I have been doing some, if albeit small martial arts practice by myself, and even one session with my daughter and other friends, so I'm not completely useless. Like I said, I am going to start to be less sedentary, and more proactive. Walking to town for example, more often at least. Public transport surely is a blessing when the buses decide to arrive on time that is, at least. But walking, one step in front of another, is truly a treasure, and one which I have been neglecting of late. I need to get more into it. Plus, I want to do some more press ups. Hell, I will do some now. Give me a minute, and let me see how many I can do…

There you go. Fifteen. Nicht schlecht. I once did Fifty. If I do them every day, I should hit this target soon. But it does gas me out. We will see.

I'm pleased that me and Will are sparring again. I have been sorely missing this aspect of live combat, and assuming I don't get any threats by my landlord, then hopefully we can continue this pattern.

I am considering asking him to start on the floor, so we can practice our groundwork.

Something we haven't been doing, as of late. With no strikes or kicks allowed. Or at least from the standing clinch. Again, with no strikes. Just the clinch, throws/takedowns, and on the ground, from the mount, to half guard for example/

I am confident if I put him in *Kesa-Gatame* (the Scarf Hold, which is the first judo hold you will learn, well it's the first I was taught anyway), he would struggle. Well today he told me that he did Judo and Wrestling at school. Which is a possibility. Because like I said, today he fended off my attacks well, leading to the draw. But you know, it could also be lies, god knows.

At least if we start on the ground, there will be no testing of

our break-fall apparatus, and it can
be dangerous falling on sheer
concrete. And instead the two of us
will have to rely on touch, and the
great Mixed Martial Art videos we
have watched, to give us
inspiration for the moves to pull.
Which should be funny, seeing as I
don't think either of us have
watched that many! Laughing out
loud.

Oh well. He's going on
holiday tomorrow, for a couple of
weeks, so that will give me, and
both of us, a chance to heal and get
our act together for the next bout.
Should be fun, and hopefully I will
be able to get it recorded next time,
as well.

41 : The Blues

I thought I had lost you. I thought I would never see you again. I thought that the time we had spent together, were over. The joy I had shared in our presence was no more. That my life was over.

The music which I'd spent the years hoping for, dreaming for, were no more.

I was close to giving up. To seeking solace elsewhere.

But then I picked up the guitar. Played a chord. Played another. Kept the hope alive in my heart, whereas elsewhere it was dead.

Kept the Blues alive, on this guitar, in this house, at this juke box.

And slowly, oh so slowly, we
were able to revive the bird from
the ashes. The legendary Phoenix,
everyone else had long given for
dead, who had closed her eyes and
said he final prayer, was once
again, able to rise from the ashes,
and like our heavenly father,
return to the Earth once more.

This simple song, with
simple notes, simple chords :
Brings back to life, the faith. The
faith of the dead and dying, and
now the faith of the children. And
the men and women.

This life we lead is often a
simple one. And at times it is
complicated, oh so heavy. Then we
move it forwards and bring it
closer to our heart. With a jukebox
and a stereo. Or a television and a

games console. A subscription, and an hour to enjoy it.

Some quality time with our loved ones, and a prayer for the dead.

And slowly, carefully, we can nurture the love we thought was dead. Spend time with her. When we can. And keep a space next to our heart, so that when we can't be together, the space is taken.

Hasn't this always been the way of man? To lament the gone, and treasure those that are still here?

For the kings and the princes, and for the queens and the princesses? They all share the stage with us.

A single life is all we are given. Please make the most of it. I should say I will see you in the next one, but it will be too late then. We shouldn't count our blessings. But make the most of this one. You only live once. And for the future? What doors will be open for us? For our children, and their children? For the rest of mankind?

Will they finally be able to close the doors to suffering and hardship, and give way to a future of hope and resilience? So, they don't have to suffer like we did? Like our parents did? And their parents?

Can the fiction of the past be finally put to bed, and make way for a future of hope and truth? Of companionship and brotherhood? Wasn't this the dream of our elders, from the French American and Portuguese revolutions?

Don't give up your dreams. I brought them here to live with me. But I couldn't hack it. Now I must work every day to keep hold of them. And when I die, I can kiss the world goodbye. I'd like to think that my life can act as a beacon for others who have suffered in the mental health system. And I am worried that the mistakes I have made, will leave a stain on my memory.

Honestly, if you have got with me this far, got with us this far, then you have done well. So, some parting words? Avoid the beer and wine, it will be the death of you. And avoid the cigarettes as well because they are also no good. Keep on doing what you are good at. If you can find someone to love,

hold on to them. Never let her/him
go.

42 : Music

I find that playing the steel strung
Spanish Acoustic Guitar, to be a
little rough on my hands. So, for
example the left hand must hold
down the strings on the notes, and
the right hand must pluck them.
Or if you are so lucky as to own a
pic, then you can strum, or pic
them, using this device. In fact,
today I purchased some pics, as
well as a Blues guitar book, and I
am feeling quite optimistic in my
music playing. Like I can push the
boat, further out in my practice
sessions. Get further along with the
practices. And learn more.

Plus, today I had my hair cut, and one of the neighbouring hairdressers commented on how much better my breathing is, then as to the old times I used to see him. I think this is true. And like I told him, I consider the fact that we seem to be on a better medication now, is a large part of why this is good. I think the meds suit me, and the fact that I am in a good place with regards to my housing and family life, all contribute to my positive health outlook.

I don't know if I told you this, but a few days ago I levelled up on Call of Duty Black Ops Three, then a private, now a middle Sergeant. Which was because I was able to get some kills in. You see in this game, on online mode, you only level up if you kill the other players. Not in real life, but on the game. And using my Kudo fully automatic machine gun, you only must line them up with the sites, and hold the right trigger down for a moment, and they are blown away.

The thing is, when I first owned this game, like a few years ago, and I played in online then, I was truly useless. And couldn't get kills in if it was the end of me. But since then I have completed the first and second Black Ops games and got better at this the third one. So for example I have progressed far enough to unlock the safe-house, and also the computer terminal and internet, which has told me about smart technology, smart materials for example, able to use camouflage as a part of the soldier's uniform. To make them blend in with the scenery. Quite exceptional.

So anyway, I was playing the game, running in to hailstorms of bullets, and catching a foe or three on the way.

Then something quite remarkable started to happen. We were playing team games, where the victor is decided by the kills, and possession of the node/orb, and I was being assigned a minder. Basically, a guardian who hold back with me, at the back, near the base, deep into our held territory, and then he or she who take care of any enemies who approached and tried to scalp me. And when that happened, I even tried to scarper, to hide, and run from the bullets. This tactic seemed to work quite well, and I think as a team, we won at least two best of three games, in this way.

The games are a team effort, and by uniting, it really felt like we were achieving something greater. Hell, I can't wait to show this new game mode to my daughter, whom I'm sure will take to it like a duck to water. I will explain to her, that if she is worried, she can just hold back, and return to safety. Hopefully she will get a guardian, in the same way I did. Nice game.

So why was I talking about this? Because believe it or not, playing Call of Duty has a connection to playing the guitar, in that they both take good hand strength, as well as good eye to hand coordination. And despite not having played much of the guitar in these last three years or so, I have been plugging away at my games. Not just Call of Duty, but also Fallout 4, which was another challenge with regards to eye to hand coordination, and hand strength. As well as the Tekken's before that.

You probably think that I'm beating around the bush. Well if you want me to talk about the recent disaster which has been my internet train wreck of recent days, I will get to that. But I must be careful over what I say. So not as to further offend anyone, and so I can try to set the record straight, with regards to my position in the field. Once and for all.

43 :

Where do we come from? Where are we
going when we die?
Who gives us our freedoms? Who brings us
together?

God is all these things. His love
provides for us, in the cold, in the dark,
after bereavement. He does not judge. He
does not blame. He provides us a light in
the darkness. Hope when it is all done.

We need God. He has lots of
different names. God, Jesus, Jehovah,
Mother Nature, Sophia, and Allah. We need
love. He is our friendships. He is our
health. He is our love.

Without God we have nothing. And
alone in a barren universe, we are but
atoms which bounce into one another.
Terminal, finite, limited, closed, and
stopped. With God we have harmony, we
have union, we have hope, we have wealth
we have a future.

God is in all of us. From the moment
you take your first breath, to when you sigh
your last. He is there. He was there for you,
and he will stay there till the end. He knew

you before you were born, and he will stay with you when you die. Right by your side.

Believe it or not my books are a chance for me to pay homage to him. To spend time with the written word, to seek out the truth, to find allies in my readers, and negate the dark forces of Satan in advance.

Please stay with me. And if you have got this far, you certainly have done. Sometimes we forget to honour our parents. Our grandparents and our heavenly father. We continue through live as driving on autopilot. Not bothered by the other road or pavement users. We need to take heed. And consider that our every action, and every reaction, has already been written. God gave us freewill. Which enables us to take hold of our lives and craft a destiny. He also gave us companionship, and family, which gives us goals and friendships and hope. He loves us.

As a child I was without God. I went to a secular school and came from a heritage of strict Atheism. It wasn't until after I have spent many months in hospital, that I

274

discovered the hospital chapel. And the hope I found in prayer there, as well as songs of praise, opened a new spiritual dimension to my life, I never knew was possible.

I don't like these street preachers, who shut down their verses, down our ears, as if their faith is the only one. Each person has their own conviction and truth. Each person, man woman and even children, are free to build their own connection with our creators. We may not like it; we may not be able to look him in the eyes but remember that we are remembered. That we are praised, and we are loved. And just as every mother loves the new-born babes, so too God loves us.

Industry, and work are admirable qualities if you can produce them. All our companionships, unions, hopes, are listened to. God will and does provide justice for all our misdemeanours. And just as Tony Blair, must pay with his conscience for the million innocent civilians he killed in Iraq, and you can see he is a broken man, haunted by this fact. So too we all must pay for our crime.

I nearly lost my wife and kid. I am still holding on to them but find it hard to do so. My god provides me with contact with them, and gives me a future, whereas the annihilation of a strictly non forgiving justice system, would have long thrown away the key to my jail cell. I'm lucky they didn't charge me.

I like to think that it is because of the strength of my relationship with the girls, that the years I have supported them, both here in the United Kingdom, and when they were over in Africa, stood for something. That the strength of the foundations we have built in our lives, mean something, and that it is not just them, but our forefathers and mothers in heaven, who can speak up for me in the eternal judgment.

Yet I know that our support workers, and justices, also will have exercised caution, both in their decision to separate them from me, for their safety, as well as that of others. And, to give me a lifeline and future, in giving me contact with them here forth.

I am also very aware that I am on my final warning. Perhaps I have passed it? And as every good yarn needs a strong beginning, closure is also needed. So, am I ready to give up on them? Not yet. I am still trying.

44 :

BANG

The lights went out. Slowly I came to. But I couldn't move. My body was fixed. Tied to a bed. I could hear, just about. I remember my mother sitting by my side. Every day. In hospital. In Intensive care.

I was in a coma. All my fears, true. Realized. All my hopes, my ambitions, my dreams, dropped.

There was nothing. Only darkness. I had a tube up my throat and down my soldier.

I couldn't breathe. I couldn't wee. I couldn't speak.

They did a life test on me. I got a three. We thought that was close to death. Negative.

Three is the lowest on the scale I found out later. I was in effect, dead.

And so how did I come back? Mainly through the love of my mum. The woman who suckled me and stood by my side through the hell of years I endured at school. Where I only survived through nightly excursions on my personal computer. Playing games.

But here I was at life's edge. And fighting for my life. This was a difficult period for me. And the day our good princess died, was the day I walked again. Laat maar zitten.

I made it. Someone who thinks they have done something, don't know the meaning of trial, until they have faced coma.

So, when I was there on that bed, do I remember what happened to me. After twenty-three years? The day I died, but my parents didn't turn off the machines. I was given another chance at life. The chance to turn my life around.

To fall in love. To become a parent. To write books. What's up with that?

And they complain when I haven't been able to hold down jobs? When I am not very good at keeping my flat tidy.

That I struggle to maintain a good sex drive.

So, I surround myself with people that love me. With people that have experienced a single per cent of the pain I have suffered. And I have recovered. Slowly

The coma stays with me. I get cold hands, even a cold bum. I am on such a high dose of medication, that they must keep me on the ward for three hours after each jab. And it is a mean big old needle that goes in my bum.

But I am out of that now. I am a survivor. I have the love of a good woman and her child, something that many others will never have, and I am grateful.

I must temper my actions. Remember the good will and prayers, that kept me alive in my darkest hour. Not to mention the sacrifices given to me by my mum, dad, and sister, for every friend who came to visit me in hospital, and every neighbour that said a prayer when I was that close to death. God bless them.

45 : Daisy the Cat i

Daisy was a cat. She was a very special cat. She was rescued as a young cat, from a house where they had a lot of cats. And the owners didn't treat them very well. Daisy had lots of brothers and sisters and was always fighting with them for food. Plus, the owners treated them as animals, not giving them individual love. And so, in this way, the early formative years of her life were quite cruel and harsh.

One day the owners decided to get rid of her. And she was lucky, that her new owners, JoJo, and family, agreed to take her in. But after being transported to her new address, she was scared. In fact, she was terrified. So, for this reason, the minute she was taken out of the cat box from the car journey (and like most other cats, she *hated* being in that box in the car), she immediately ran to safety. Hiding away in the corners of the living room. Behind the sofas, deep into the corners of the room. And no amount of gentle "here kitty kitty", would coax her out of this abyss.

JoJo and his daughter used to leave food for her on plates. And little by little, steady by steady, the food would go missing. At night, the plate would have cat food on it, either the biscuits, or as she preferred the jelly, and in the morning the food wouldn't be there. At first daughter thought there had been a thief in the house.

How dare they enter the premise and steal this poor kitten din dins. But how could this be? They always locked the doors and checked the windows were secure. So how could this be happening. But then, slowly over the coming days, Daisy would start to show her face. She became stronger, and more confident as the days rolled into weeks. Showing more and more of her black and white fur. Gaining new confidence in JoJo and daughter. So that eventually she would even come out from hiding, and eat, and even watch tv with the owners.

They say cats have nine lives. I think Daisy has had some of hers, given what I put her through! But even today, Daisy is still a much-loved cat. With a strength, only distinctive to her mum and aunty.

She would catch mice, and the odd bird. In fact, she used to like it when JoJo trailed a string, in front of her. So, she could catch that, it's a feline reflex, to catch the mice. And together with her new owners, she used to spend many happy days, chasing these imaginary mice.

Once she caught fleas. And this was a problem. The local supermarket sold special cat de-flea potion, which you had to rub a little bit behind her ears, and it was supposed to deal with this problem. Well they did that, and it did after a few days, clear the problem. But by that time the house was pretty much infested with fleas. And only repeated cleaning, hovering, and wiping the surfaces down, would eventually deal with this problem. In fact, Daisy was cured of the fleas, a long time before they had left the house altogether.

Cats are different from dogs. Whereas a dog is loyal and a companion, cats are more independent. I'm not saying you can't make friends with cats. God help us, are well looked after cat is a good friend, much in the way a well-fed dog can be. But it takes time. And if you compare the noises they make, a dog barks, which is like a little more aggressive, to a cat's meow. Which is more subtle. But they are clever, and they can understand quite a lot of human speech. If not at first, they pick this up over time.

Daisy was a good cat. And as I have said already, she was a special cat. She needed this inner strength and fortitude, to survive the challenge, which was to occur a few years on. When she was locked in the house, without food or water, for a matter of three weeks (or more). But whereas any other pet, would have died from this trauma, Daisy survived. She wasn't happy. She did nearly die. And when after those three/four weeks the front door finally opened, she shot out faster than a bullet on speed. And JoJo would never see her again.

But she returned eventually to my daughter, and finally settled in their new home. Which was another home, another flat. A brand-new start.

JoJo was sorry that he had left her alone in this way. At the time he wasn't right in his head. He had been going through a very difficult period. And this had terminated in his apprehension and detention by the powers that be, followed by a police arrest, a period of sleeping rough on the street, and a violent knockout blow. As well as having thrown the keys he had for that old flat, down the drain. So that even if had wanted to save Daisy, this was out of his hands.

He was transferred from the police holding cell, to a secure locked psychiatric ward (again), and Daisy was alone. No more imaginary cats to play with, no tastier cat food, or cooling water to drink. She was left to die. She thought the whole world had forgotten about her. And as the hours rolled into days, and the days in two weeks, she had almost given up hope. But then returned to her. She was fed and watered, and eventually brought back to health.

But she vowed she would never forgive me for this, what he had done to her. Even though, he didn't consider himself fully responsible for this animal cruelty, in that it was first the police, and then after the hospital, which had detained him, and prevented him from saving Daisy, she was still his ward, and his responsibility.

And it wasn't just Daisy, but the cats of the world, which took this blow. But as I said already, she grew stronger, and back to health eventually. And even if JoJo did never get to meet her again in person, she was able to show him photos of her progress, and so he still loved her, even if this was only one way.

46 : Daisy the Cat ii

The next day was grim outside. It was dark, and it was cold. JoJo felt tired. He wasn't sure how long he had been sitting in the chair for, much less how much longer he would be there. He felt tired, and thirsty.

A moment later the door opened, and two uniformed officers entered.

"JoJo, are you okay?"

"I'm fine".

"Would you like a glass of water?"

He hesitated, and then shrugged his shoulders.

"Sure"

The sound of a toilet flushing, and a beat later one of the officers re-entered holding a white Styrofoam cup.

"Here you go..."

"Thanks" JoJo mumbled, took the fine beverage, and downed the lotion in one.

"Now what do you want to ask me today?"

"JoJo" the officer continued, "remember you are here of your own free will. At any point you can choose to end the interview and walk out of our office. You haven't been charged, and you are still a free man!"

"So If I choose to walk out now, I'd get as far as the exit... you wouldn't arrest me then, you wouldn't rugby tackle me to the ground, and give me an acuphase depot injection, to make me fall asleep until the next day?"

"No, we wouldn't".

"You're a liar officer. I know this game, as much as anyone, I know the consequences of acting deviant to the norm. Of thinking outside of the box. Of breaking the law. And that's why I'm here!"

"Are you sure you don't want a solicitor present?" The first officer queried; you are more than welcome to have one here?"

"No, it's okay" JoJo muttered. I know what I've done, I know why I'm here. Let's get this over with…"

"Okay JoJo. You say you don't know anything about that body we found in your garden, in your shed. What about this…" and the officer pushed forwards a photo across the table. "Do you know who this is?"

With difficulty JoJo reached for the photo and drew it closer to him. Straining to view in the grim light of the artificial luminous which flooded the room. It could be anytime, night or day. He had been here for at least twenty-four hours since this latest arrest, and the world was beginning to become peaky. His eyes struggled to focus in this scenario. Then he saw it…

"But that's Daisy officer? Daisy the cat!"

"Correct. When did you last see her?"

"Well it was only a few days ago, say a week, and she was fine. Oh damn. I left her alone in the house, without fresh food or water, for a good week, since I have been seeing all this call girls. Damn. I hope she's okay. Where did you get this photo?"

"Where we got the photo is of no relevance. What is relevant is the point that she has gone missing. It has been over two weeks since your arrest, and when you dad Pierre went in to look for the cat, she wasn't there. We are worried for her safety!"

"Damn she's not there… Do you think an animal can survive for two weeks without food and water? Damn she could be dead?"

"Well if it's any reassurance we didn't find a carcass. We wanted to know if you know where she is?"

"I suppose she shot out the door when dad opened it. Hopefully she will make the way back to her carers, in her own time. She must have lost a lot of weight and grown some new grey hairs given this trauma!"

"You're lucky we don't charge you with animal neglect, to go with your litany of other offenses I hope you realize?"

"Okay. Well I promise you I didn't touch her. And God knows where she is. But we did let her out, from time to time. She used to come back covered in fleas, which then proceeded to infest the house, and were a nightmare to eradicate, not to mention the expensive lotions and creams we tried applying to her, to kill the damn things! No, I

swear officer I have no idea where she is now! Next question?"
"That will do for today" the police inspector concluded.

47 : Daisy the Cart iii

The next day JoJo found himself back in the interrogation chamber. Sitting on the chair across from him was Daisy. Daisy the cat. She didn't speak but had mind powers. And was able to transmit her thoughts to him telepathically.

"Hi Daisy. It's good to see you again. It's been a long time..."
HOW DARE YOU JOJO. YOU LEFT ME FOR DEAD?! I WAS IN YOUR CARE, AND YOU ABANDONED ME. YOU CAN TAKE YOUR FAKE MICE, AND

EAT IT, AS FAR AS I AM
CONCERNED!

"I'm sorry Daisy" JoJo tried. "I
didn't mean for it to end this way. I
was unwell. I placed the
desperation of psychosis, above
your health and safety. I didn't
mean for this to happen. Please
forgive me?"
NOT FORGIVEN. HOW COULD
YOU? HOW COULD YOU?

"Please forgive me Daisy. I
didn't want it to end this way?"
I WILL NEVER FORGIVE YOU.
AND JUST AS YOU LEFT YOUR
FAMILY, YOU LEFT ME AS
WELL! YOU SHOULD BE IN
PRISON NOW. FOR ANIMAL
NEGLECT/ABUSE, AND THAT'S
SAYING NOTHING OF YOUR
OTHER CRIMES YOU ARE SO
PROUD OF!

"Okay Daisy. Like I said I am sorry. Both for you and the other stuff. I suppose you are right, talking about it helps get it off my chest. But it's more than that. I'm not afraid of the truth. It is one of my weaknesses, and strengths. I find that by being honest I am able to breathe the air of the God's." YOU LEFT ME FOR DEAD, AND YOU ALSO ABANDONED YOUR FAMILY. WHAT KIND OF A MAN DO YOU CALL THAT? LISTEN MISTER, YOU THINK IT'S OVER? YOU THINK SOME PETTY APOLOGIES CAN UNDO THE DAMAGE YOU HAVE DONE?

"I don't know how I can ever make it up to you. Maybe if I buy you some more cat treats? That would be a start, right?"

CAT NIP? WHAT? WHAT ARE YOU TALKING ABOUT? WHEN WAS THE LAST TIME YOU PLACED SOMEONE ELSE ABOVE YOURSELF? YOU ARE THE MOST SELF CENTERED AND EGOTISTICAL/NARCISSISTIC HUMAN I HAVE EVER KNOWN, AND I HAVE KNOWN A LOT OF THEM!

"Sorry Daisy. I know you are a good cat. Maybe the best. And I won't forget you. I don't know how long you have left, a good decade yet I hope. And just as I have taken a vow never to sleep with another woman again, so too I will honour the love I have for you. I will get you that catnip. That will be a start. I will be careful in all the fights I get in, never to hurt the opponent.

So, if it's Will, I can throw some punches at him. The same as he will throw them at me. And it is good to raise up the heat of our battles, so just like a good game of chess, we are both operating at a capacity that will test ourselves, without causing lasting damage. The martial arts I've done, have prepared the foundation for these contests. But it is the actual practice of live combat, all be it not to hurt, which where we can both raise the level of our capacity and capabilities, form normal to special?"

SPECIAL? YOU SURE ARE THAT? YOU CONSIDER BEATING UP YOUR FRIENDS ANOTHER BLESSED PASTIME, TO BOAST TO THE WORLD? WHERE IS THE TRAINING YOU

DID THAT TEACHES YOU
NEVER TO USE YOUR MARTIAL
SKILLS TO ATTACK? TO KEEP
THEM STRICTLY WITHIN THE
SACROSANCT WALLS OF THE
DOJO, IN WHICH THEY WERE
FIRST SHOWED YOU?
"I know daisy. I know I was taught
that. And I also know that if my
old instructors find that I have
been practicing my martial arts
skills on the street, they would be
horrified. But hold on a minute
hear me out.
The same as I have had to use
martial arts for self-defence, on
some occasions gone, I really feel
that I am ready to take it to the
next level. Like I said, I won't hurt
him. But I am getting better, and
stronger.

We need to take it to the next level. For a start, I'm not going to wear my slippers the next time I spar with him. That was giving him too much of a handicap. I will wear my trainers, to give me more leverage to my strikes and kicks. I am hoping to watch some more of my martial arts DVDs at some point. I find the ideas within, to be a good source of knowledge for these fights.

SO WHY ARE YOU TELLING ME THIS? WHAT DO YOU HOPE TO GAIN BY SHARING THIS NONSENSE WITH ME? IT'S LIKE YOUR DAD SAYS, MARTIAL ARTS ONLY LEAD YOU TO TROUBLE. IT IS IMMERSING IN A FALSE FANTASY WORLD, A WORLD OF NINJAS AND BLACK BELTS,

WHICH TIME HAS PROVED
TIME AND TIME AGAIN, TO BE
SIGNS OF A RELAPSE!

"Please forgive me Daisy. I
know what you are saying. Like
when my dad said, 'martial arts
only lead to trouble'. I can see
where you get this conclusion
from. I really can. But it's not just
that. It's so much more. Martial arts
are, to my mind, an avenue to
develop your self-worth and
power, above the range of the
standard normal civilian life, and
on to that of a fighter, and warrior,
and honourable Samurai. The
honour, which world war two so
very nearly saw the eclipse of. And
this treasure, like the box in
Chinese drawn around the
precious jewels of language, to
signify just that. They are treasures.

Our babies, we need to protect and honour. The Bu of Budo. The Aiki of Aikido. Please trust me I am going to put my all in to honouring my wife and kid, and hope that the worst is over."

YAP YAP. HAVE YOU FINISHED?

"Just one more thing Daisy. I want to build on my successes, what precious few I have had, to move forwards. Yes, that means trying out new ideas. Taking risks, much as like my multi-fold hospital admissions have, on the total of it, taught me a lot of more valuable lessons. And my martial art, JoJutsu, or Jodo, or whatever you want to call it... Well It's not just about attack and defence, although granted that is a part. And it's not just about being able to take an

302

attack before you can throw one. But it is also about entering, surviving, and ultimately triumphing over the mental health apparatus, which sadly still exists here in the United Kingdom, and across the world. The ability to ride the tiger and walk away pride intact.

You can't beat them Daisy. Not on your own. You must team up. Make friends, and allies. Build a castle, starting with the foundations. Complete with a moat. Which will stand the test of time.

I'VE HEARD ENOUGH. NEVER TALK TO ME AGAIN!

48 : I'm Sorry Daisy iv

"Okay Daisy. I'm sorry for leaving you in the house when I went astray. I'm sorry about shouting at my wife. I'm sorry about touching my stepdaughter's chest.

I did wrong. I was a fool. I thought I could take on the world. I thought I could do I degree. I thought I could be better than my (nearly separated wife). I thought I could be my nineteen-year-old self, in the bones of this thirty-eight-year-old me. Ik had het fout.

I have been trying to juice out lengthy essays for each of these chapters, so please bear with me.

I've now got half of the world hating me, and the other half ignoring me. The few friends I have left, are mostly mentally ill like me.

I am lucky that my wife continues to let me be a part of her life. She is quite withing rights, to cut me from her life altogether. And it's only because we go back a long way, and I think she knows inside that it was a mistake and will not be repeated. Ever.

So, I'm sorry please believe me. I will continue to pay child support, for as long as they need it. And what I can't provide with my body, I will try the best to ameliorate with my soul. That was the problem.

And my punishment? Well I must take a drug, once a month. Which strips me of my sex drive. And makes it impossible for me to make love. Have you ever tried doing it, or even playing on a soft soldier? It isn't easy. And this is for the foreseeable future. Or another good ten years at least. Damn it. But I suppose I deserve it. And I am lucky to not be locked up for good. Other people have been for less crimes.

So, what now? To continue to support my wife and daughter as best I can. To keep up the weekly contact. And child support. To keep on pushing my daughter to achieve to her very best. To reach the sky in this life, which the earth only too often, feels far too grounded. To support my wife, as best as I can, for as long as I can. To never sleep with another woman, for as long as I live. To never do it with another person again.

I need to stop giving my heart out to strangers on the street.

For whilst it may be true, that we are all only one letter away from, meeting them there. So too, we don't know who we can trust.

It is easy to make fake friends when you have money. But trust me, not everyone should be trusted. And that precious prize, friendship, can readily be stripped.

But enough playing games. Yesterday when I called you up on the phone, and you heard my voice over speakerphone, you said meow. Now I think that was your way of saying, you understand, and you forgive me.

God bless you Daisy.

49 : Nearly There

Okay, So, you have got with us this far. You have nearly come to the end.

In this book you have taken JoJo's hand, as he visited friends, got in to fights, entered and subsequently left locked hospital wards, saw off more than one attempt on his life, and struggled with a possibly lifelong mental illness.

We have watched how JoJo reacts under the stress of interrogation, torture, moments of great success, as well as more than a few losses. And then back into the safety of his armchair.

You have heard about his successes with his small family. How he completed his degree, and advice he give to the world, but specifically the next generation, on tips how they can complete theirs.

His ongoing struggle with the martial arts. Including fights, he has been in, some won, some drawn, but mostly losses.

You have witnessed through the eyes of this fictional character how he has battled smoking, spending a total of fifteen years in and out of hospital. How he used the time between these breaks, to attempt to make something of his life. From taking a two-year part-time Access course at his local university, on to the degree. And after that a short-lived voluntary job. Short lived, because it was interrupted with, yet another breaks down, and yet another lengthy hospital stays.

You have stayed by his side as he travelled to London, to partake in a mental health forum. Of how his love for computer games, fighting zombies and listening to great music, have helped him while away the hours he isn't sleeping. How his contact has been the only thing keeping him sane, in this world of madness.

And how in-between his moments of madness and violence, love and comradeship have kept him grounded.

I hope you have enjoyed reading this book. It has taken me the best part of a year to write, and I have truly laid my soul bare to the world, in its creation.

Whilst JoJo is a fictional character which gives me some liberty and license of fictitious work. But I have kept true to my conscience, and relayed real events, real people, and real moments of my life. Moments of time, that *really* happened!

Thanks for reading, and God bless you!

Johnnie

50 : Closure

Okay JoJo. We've heard your stories. And had time to make judgment on your situation.

You are still a young man. You have a wife that loves you, and a daughter who looks up to you.

Sure, you have made mistakes in the past. Talking to the

wrong people, making friends, and at times being taken advantage of when you were vulnerable.

You have wasted money in the past, on things you then called investments, and this whilst everyone else told you to avoid.

You have spent your life chasing dreams young man. And whilst this is not something that many of us would choose to do, that has been your calling.

Yet rather than crumble and fold when the heat was on you, you held true to your dream. You held on to the love of god, and the hope of providence.

So, when the nights rolled in two months and the months into years, still you were here. Your hairs a little greyer and your walk a little slower.

Good friends are best remembered in our hearts and our dreams. For whilst those that have left us, will never again share a wine, they will always be with us, if we remember them.

And this applies to all our friends, our heroes, and our elders.

I don't know what else to say to you JoJo. Other than you are free to go. Please remember the moments you have shared with us under these locked walls. We have taught you, but equally you have taught us. Taught us to mind what we say and consider what we do. Both before and after. Don't take this the wrong way, but I hope that I never see you again. You are above these institutions. Mind what you say, and what we do, protect those you love, and have a good life! Bye-bye JoJo!

New Ending :
    Look JoJo today we will let you from your cramped cell, and on to face the music. Please promise me that you won't say a word of this to no man. And let us remember that you have come a long way. A long way from those days of punching the walls, or your family members. I don't think that I don't know. I look above you, before you behind you and below you. I know what you are thinking even before you say it. And there are some things that I cannot forgive.
    But enough about me, what about you? Did you like our conversations, the way I always

314

asked you for the truth, and then waited to listen for your explanation. And whilst I may not always have agreed with you, we can settle on this one thing, that everyone is different, and as we move forwards in to this heavenly and by all means perfect realm, let us hold our heads high and not be afraid. We can make it if we try and find hope and salvation where once there was none.

As I said before I will not always be here for you. There will come a time when you are the candle bearer, for the future of your next generations. This is the way of the world, of mankind and the future, we all must work towards?

And will one day mankind extend from the heavenly

barricades of this planet and seek extra-terrestrial refuge? Well for that one I can't be sure. None of us know what the future may bring. From a conflagration of mystique to a morass of problems, we could go up and we can go down. Without an anchor a boat can't park, and without a rudder it can't steer.

So, in this way we need each other, for comfort and peace. Safety and restoration.

Please heed my words. Move forwards when you can and remember to eat sleep and breathe. Together we can make it, and then this will be our final communion. Please take heed of my stories, for one day it may be all you have left.